Farewell, Dawn

**Other books by
Ann M. Martin**

Rachel Parker, Kindergarten Show-off
Eleven Kids, One Summer
Ma and Pa Dracula
Yours Turly, Shirley
Ten Kids, No Pets
Slam Book
Just a Summer Romance
Missing Since Monday
With You and Without You
Me and Katie (the Pest)
Stage Fright
Inside Out
Bummer Summer

BABY-SITTERS LITTLE SISTER series
THE BABY-SITTERS CLUB mysteries
THE BABY-SITTERS CLUB series

Farewell, Dawn

Ann M. Martin

AN
APPLE
PAPERBACK

SCHOLASTIC INC.
New York Toronto London Auckland Sydney

Cover art by Hodges Soileau

ISBN 0-590-22872-2

12 11 10 9 8 7 6 5 4 3 2 1   5 6 7 8 9/9 0/0

Printed in the U.S.A.   40

First Scholastic printing, August 1995

*The author gratefully acknowledges
Suzanne Weyn
for her help in
preparing this manuscript.*

Farewell, Dawn

CHAPTER 1

I was lying on a pink sand beach. Warm sun streamed down over me and the white surf tickled my bare toes. Stretching lazily, I sat up and looked out to sea. Pods of dolphins leapt in graceful arches as they swam by. In the distant water, circling gulls called my name. "Dawn . . . Dawn . . . Dawn . . ."

Well . . . not exactly.

But that's what I had been dreaming when I opened my eyes on Monday morning and was met by the blinding glare of full sunshine in my face. And those gulls now sounded an awful lot like my best friend and stepsister, Mary Anne.

"Dawn!" I heard her call. As I sat up in bed, Mary Anne rapped at my room door and walked in. "I can't believe you're still in bed," she cried. "You're supposed to baby-sit for Sara and Norman Hill at nine and it's after eight now."

Mary Anne knew my summertime schedule not only because she's an incredibly organized person, but because she's the secretary of the BSC, otherwise known as the Baby-sitters Club. But I'll tell you about it a little later.

"I almost overslept!" I gasped, throwing off my sheet.

"I'm sitting for the Braddocks today, so I'll walk with you for part of the way," Mary Anne offered as she smoothed her hair in my mirror. She was already dressed in blue and white plaid shorts and a blue T-shirt.

I pulled on a pair of white shorts and a short-sleeved flowered blouse, slipped into straw sandals, bent forward, then quickly brushed my long blonde hair. "Ready!" I announced, tossing my hair back over my shoulders.

"Dad's making eggs," Mary Anne told me.

"Cool! I'm starving," I said.

Although meals don't always go smoothly in my family, breakfasts aren't usually too bad. In fact, eggs is one of the few foods our entire family can agree on. (Pancakes and hot cereal are okay, too, but Mom thinks Richard puts too much sugar in them.)

You see, Mom and I eat nothing but healthy foods. We never eat junk food or red meat. Mary Anne and Richard eat the way most Americans do (which is pretty *un*healthy, if you ask me). But, we can enjoy eggs together once in a while. (Mom says they're too high in fat if you eat them all the time.)

When Mary Anne and I reached the kitchen, Richard was just dishing some eggs from a frying pan onto Mom's plate. I tried to ignore the gross, fatty, bubbling bacon still sizzling on the stove. Even the smell of it is disgusting to me.

"Good morning," Mom said cheerfully.

"Eggs, girls?" Richard offered. Peeking into the pan, I saw he'd added bits of tomatoes and cheese to the eggs. They looked terrific.

"Sure," I said, pulling two plates from the cupboard and handing one to Mary Anne.

"Do you think we could go to the beach this weekend?" Mary Anne asked.

"I don't know," said Richard as he sat down. "It's going to be pretty crowded."

I let out a long sigh. Back in California we went to the beach almost every weekend. Here in Connecticut, where the beaches are smaller, they get way overcrowded in no time.

I'm originally from Palo City, a suburb of Anaheim, California. We (Mom, my younger brother Jeff, and I) moved here when I was in the seventh grade.

Mom grew up in Stoneybrook, but went to college in California, which was where she met my dad. After they divorced, I guess Mom wanted to be closer to her parents (who are my grandparents, of course). So we moved to Stoneybrook and bought this really old farmhouse. (And I do mean old! It was built in 1795.)

Jeff, who is ten now, didn't take well to living in Stoneybrook. He missed Dad, he couldn't get used to the cold weather, and he missed his friends. So he made the painful decision to move back to California and live with Dad.

I know how Jeff felt, because earlier this year I started feeling the same way. I started missing Dad, California, and my friends.

Don't get me wrong. There are lots of things I *love* about living here in Stoneybrook. I get along great with Mom. (She's kind of messy and scatterbrained but that doesn't bother me. I'm used to it.) Richard is a wonderful stepdad, and Mary Anne is the best.

I even like our house, though on cold, windy nights it does seem eerie and creaky with its small rooms, low ceilings, and uneven, shadowy corners. But it's a pretty cool house. There's even a secret passage that runs from my bedroom to the barn out back! (How's that for spooky?)

Plus, there's the BSC with all my good friends who belong to it and the adorable kids we sit for. They've become a big, important part of my life here in Stoneybrook.

Still . . . there's something about Palo City. It's home, too, and it just sort of calls to me in a way that's hard to explain. Dad and Jeff are there and so are the friends I grew up with.

Besides that, Dad just remarried. At first I didn't like Carol, his new wife. But during my last visit there I changed my mind. She's pretty cool. I'd like to know her even better.

With all the people in Palo City who are so important to me, I can't get this longing to be there out of my head or my heart.

That was why I went back for a long visit earlier this year. I never intended to stay, I just wanted to be there for a while.

"We've got to go," Mary Anne said to me when we had finished eating.

We cleared our dishes, said good-bye to our parents, who were leaving for work, and headed out the door. Mary Anne and I walked down Burnt Hill Road (where we live). We talked a little but mostly we were quiet. (Mary Anne and I do so many things together that, after awhile, we don't have anything new to tell each other.) That's all right. I don't think people who are close have to gab every second of the day. Sometimes, just being together is good enough.

At Slate Street, Mary Anne turned off and headed toward the Braddocks' house. I con-

tinued on for another ten minutes to the Hills'
modern-looking house. When I rang the bell,
seven-year-old Norman answered the door.

"Hi, Dawn," he said cheerfully. I didn't
want to make a big thing of it, but I was
pleased to see that Norman looked a bit thin-
ner than the last time I'd seen him.

"Looking good, Norman," I said as I
stepped into the front hall.

He smiled brightly at me. I'm sure he knew
what I was referring to. When we first started
sitting for the Hills, Norman was pretty fat.
This was a real problem because the kids in
school were teasing him (calling him Enor-
mous Hill and mean things like that). Plus,
being overweight is unhealthy. But Norman
had become determined to lose weight and
now, as I looked at him standing there, I'd
describe him as husky rather than fat.

Mr. and Mrs. Hill came to the door dressed
in lightweight jogging suits. "Dawn!" said
Mrs. Hill. "Nice to see you. We'll be at the
Fitness Faze Health Club. The number's on
the refrigerator. We shouldn't be more than
three hours at the most." The Hills work at
home (she's an artist's representative, he's a
computer systems analyst) so they're around
most days.

Mrs. Hill kissed Norman on the top of his

blond, wispy hair. " 'Bye, Normy-pie," she said.

Mr. Hill, who is a tall, balding man with broad shoulders, just smiled at me as he grabbed his gym bag from the front hall. "Be good, Norman," he said, following Mrs. Hill out the front door.

Sitting for the Hills went pretty easily that day. Sara, Norman's nine-year-old sister, played in her room with her neighbor Elizabeth for most of the time. Norman showed me his new computer game, which we played again and again. Before I knew it, the Hills were back.

By three that afternoon, I was home alone and not quite sure what to do next. Feeling hungry, I started preparing a salad from lettuce, tomatoes, alfalfa bean sprouts, and an avocado. Something about that avocado started me thinking about California.

I knew that with the three-hour time difference it was just around noon there. I wondered what my friend Sunny Winslow was doing. I could easily picture her, with her strawberry blonde hair, upturned, freckled nose, and friendly, carefree style.

Maybe she was heading out to a baby-sitting job. She'd started her own West Coast version of the BSC called the We ♥ Kids Club. It's run in a much more relaxed, casual way than the BSC, but it works for them. (When I was out there last I joined and helped them get a *little* more organized.)

If Sunny weren't baby-sitting, she might be at the beach already. She loves to hang out there or at the surf shop and chat with the boys. Sunny can be so flirty that I just want to die when I'm with her. But there's so much friendliness in her flirtiness that she manages to make it seem okay.

As I scooped the avocado pulp into my salad, I had another thought that made me bite my lower lip. What if Sunny was at the hospital?

Not long ago I learned that Sunny's mother was diagnosed with lung cancer. Mrs. Winslow is a potter who makes unbelievably beautiful stoneware. She's also one of the warmest, nicest people I've ever met. Sunny and I have been best friends since we were in second grade. I think of Mrs. Winslow as a second mother.

I glanced at the kitchen phone on the wall. Normally, I'm not supposed to call California without at least checking with Mom or Richard first. But I was dying to know how Mrs. Winslow was doing. If I had to, I'd offer to pay for the call with the money I'd just earned baby-sitting for the Hills.

I punched in Sunny's phone number, then waited, hoping she'd be there. After three rings, I heard a familiar voice say: "Sunny Daydream Winslow speaking. For the daily surf report, press one . . . now!"

"Sunny!" I cried. That was Sunny all the way, always kidding around.

"Dawn!" Sunny screamed, recognizing my voice.

We both screamed for a few more seconds, then calmed down. "Why are you calling?" she asked, suddenly concerned. "Is everything all right?" She was probably worried because I usually call in the evening when the phone rates are lower.

"No, I'm fine. I was just missing you and wondering how your mom is feeling."

"I'm cool, but Mom is still in the hospital."

I took a deep breath so my voice wouldn't shake. "How's she doing?"

"Better," Sunny replied thoughtfully. "The doctor said she hopes Mom can come home next week."

"That's great."

"Yeah, it is," Sunny agreed, but her voice was quiet and unsure. "I mean, she's not definitely coming. They have to run more tests and all. She doesn't look so great to me but maybe that's just because she's so bummed out from being in the hospital."

More than anything else I wished I could be at Sunny's house that very second to put my arm around her shoulder. It's hard to be there for a good friend when you're not *there* in person and have no hope of even getting there soon.

"That stinks," I said sympathetically. "Tell her I hope she feels better soon."

"So how are you?" Sunny asked cheerfully, changing the serious mood along with the subject.

"Everything's fine here, but do you ever wish you could be two places at once?"

"Sure. Wherever I am I always wish there was another one of me who could be at the beach."

That made me laugh. "Well, I wish one of me could be here and another one could be in California."

"Are you coming back?" Sunny asked, sounding hopeful.

"No," I told her. "But I'd sure like to come, at least for awhile."

Sunny and I talked some more, mostly about the kids I used to sit for when I was part of the We ♥ Kids Club. The more we talked, the more I longed to be there.

Finally, I said good-bye and sat down at the kitchen table with my salad. As I ate, a frightening realization came to me. At first, I didn't want to think about it and just kept pushing it out of my head.

But the insistent thought kept coming back. There was no getting away from it.

As much as I loved living in Stoneybrook, I wanted to move back to California.

Permanently.

CHAPTER 2

By five-thirty, when it was time for our Monday BSC meeting, I was really looking forward to it. I needed something to take my mind off California. I was driving myself crazy thinking about it.

"Hi, guys," I greeted Claudia Kishi and Stacey McGill as I walked into Claudia's bedroom. We always hold meetings in Claudia's room.

Claudia and Stacey were sitting on Claudia's bed looking at a picture drawn on a sketchpad. "Hi, Dawn," said Claudia. She held up the sketchpad for me to see. "What do you think of this? Does it look like her or not?"

"Wow!" I said, taking the pad from Claudia. She'd done a pastel of Stacey and it *did* look a lot like her. Not only had she recreated Stacey's large blue eyes, delicate features, and permed blonde hair, but she'd also captured something of the inner Stacey. Lately, I'm not so sure who the inner Stacey is. She's changing so much. Still, there was an expression on the sketch that definitely belonged to Stacey alone.

"Do you honestly think it looks like me?" Stacey wondered aloud. "Is my nose really that big?"

"Your nose doesn't look big at all," I said, not knowing what she was talking about. "It's not big in real life or in the sketch."

Stacey took the sketch from me and studied it carefully. "I guess it's a good likeness," she said uncertainly. "It's certainly a good sketch." She sighed deeply. "It must be great to have talent."

"You have talents," Claudia said as she dug behind the pillow on her bed and pulled out a cellophane bag of Cheez Doodles. Claud is a junk food nut. Her parents forbid her to eat it, so she hides it everywhere. (She also stashes Nancy Drew books around since her parents don't approve of those, either.)

"What kind of talent do I have?" asked Stacey.

"Math," Claudia replied. "You're a whiz in math."

"Big deal." Stacey scoffed.

I wondered why Stacey was so down on herself. Usually she's pretty upbeat. Maybe she was feeling uncomfortable about being back in the club. She'd only recently joined

13

the BSC again. For awhile, she had gone her own way, saying the BSC members weren't "mature" enough for her. Instead of being with us, she spent all her time with her boyfriend Robert and his friends. Now, though she still saw Robert, she'd decided the girls who hung around with his group weren't true friends of hers.

Personally, I was glad she was back. Even though Stacey seemed to be going through some personal changes that I didn't quite understand, I thought of her as a good friend. (Claudia and Stacey are *best* friends, but I still feel very close to the two of them as well.)

"Hel-lo!" our club president, Kristy Thomas, sang out as she bounced into the room and plunked herself into her usual spot on Claudia's director's chair. Soon the rest of the club members started pouring in.

This might be a good time for me to stop and tell you something about each club member. After that, I'll fill you in on the history of the club and how it works.

I'll start with Stacey, since you already know something about her. Like me, Stacey isn't originally from Stoneybrook. She's from New York City, and it shows. She has great taste in clothing and always knows what's in style — or what's about to become trendy any sec-

pottery, jewelry-making, print-making. Everything!

Claudia can carry off her unusual fashion creations not only because they're so artistically put together, but because she happens to be totally gorgeous. She's slim with silky, long, black hair and beautiful, dark, almond eyes. (She's Japanese-American.)

The only troublesome thing about Claudia's boundless creativity is that she'd rather be doing artwork than almost anything else — which includes schoolwork. She just barely squeaks through school, doing only enough to pass. (And she can't spell to save her life.)

Claudia's parents are not pleased with her attitude toward school. It's especially hard for them to understand because Claudia's older sister, Janine, is a real genius with some kind of astronomical I.Q. They have even threatened to make Claudia drop out of the BSC unless her grades improve.

Kristy Thomas is on top of any situation that threatens the smooth running of the club. It's mostly because of her that everything runs so . . . well, smoothly (usually). It's this quality of being in charge that has earned Kristy a reputation for being bossy.

In truth, Kristy *is* bossy, but I just think of her as a person with a big personality. I can never get over the contrast between the way Kristy looks and the way she acts. Kristy is probably the shortest girl in the eighth grade. She doesn't wear trendy clothing or do anything to her straight, shoulder-length brown hair. (You might call her look "sporty.") But, despite her appearance, when she comes into a room, boy, do you notice her! That's because she just takes over. (You should have seen her when she visited me in California. She took one look at the chaos of the We ♥ Kids Club and immediately started coming up with ways to set everything straight.)

I bet Kristy developed her big personality just to survive in a family of two older brothers (Sam and Charlie) and one younger brother (David Michael). Her father abandoned them soon after David Michael was born. (What a creep.) Kristy's mother raised all her kids alone until she met and married a guy named Watson Brewer.

Then Kristy's entire family moved from their house here on Bradford Court across town to Watson's mansion. Watson is an actual millionaire. It's a good thing he lives in a mansion because a lot of people have to fit into it.

Watson has two young kids of his own from his first marriage (Karen, who is seven, and Andrew, who is four). Then, Kristy's mom and Watson adopted a little girl from Vietnam named Emily Michelle who is now two and a half. Kristy's grandmother (her mom's mom) came to live with them to help take care of Emily Michelle. Karen and Andrew live with Watson every other month and with their mother the rest of the time. They adore Kristy and she adores them back.

"Hi," said Shannon Kilbourne, who entered the room a few minutes after Kristy did. I thought that was a little odd since Shannon and Kristy are neighbors and they almost always arrive together. "I stopped to look at a computer program Janine is working on in her room," she explained. "Wow! I couldn't even follow it."

"She *is* a genius," Claudia said lightly.

Shannon may not be a genius, but she's pretty smart. At her school she's a member of the National Honor Society. (She goes to Stoneybrook Day School, though the rest of us attend Stoneybrook Middle School, otherwise known as SMS.)

Recently, we've gotten to know Shannon a lot better. She started out as an associate member, which meant she didn't come to meetings but that we called her if we had more jobs than we could handle. She became a regular full-time member because the BSC needed someone to take my spot while I was in California. After I returned, the club had so much

19

work that Shannon kept attending regular meetings as an associate member — which was a good thing because soon after that Stacey left.

Shannon is easy to like, always pleasant and reliable. She's pretty, too, with curly blonde hair, high cheekbones, and blue-blue eyes. Shannon has two younger sisters, Maria and Tiffany. And, like Kristy, she's a dog lover. In fact, after Kristy's dog died, Shannon gave her one of the Bernese mountain dog pups her family breeds.

Just then, Mary Anne came running into the room and glanced at the digital clock on Claudia's desk. It said 5:26. "Whew! I made it!" she said, panting. Kristy insists on punctuality and gets very put out if anyone is late. "Logan and I were swimming at the community center pool and I almost lost track of time," said Mary Anne breathlessly as she sat down on Claudia's bed.

Logan Bruno is Mary Anne's boyfriend. He's really nice and good-looking, with sandy blond hair and dark eyes. I like his slight southern accent, which is left over from when he lived in Kentucky. He's also an associate member of the BSC.

I've already told you a lot about Mary Anne. She was the first friend I made when I came to Stoneybrook. And she was also the one who brought me into the club. You see, before Kristy moved, she and Mary Anne were neighbors. They were also best friends. When I met them, Mary Anne and Kristy even looked alike. They were both small with brown eyes and brown hair. Neither of them had any sense of style, either. But since then, Mary Anne has cut her hair short, grown a bit past Kristy, and become more interested in clothes.

One reason Mary Anne has blossomed is Richard no longer keeps such strict control over everything she does. Marrying Mom had a lot to do with his loosening up. Before that, he was Mary Anne's only parent. Mary Anne's mom died when Mary Anne was just a baby, and Richard was very overprotective of Mary Anne.

If Mary Anne and I hadn't become friends, Mom and Richard might never have married. We were the ones who got them together. One day while looking through Mom's old yearbook we discovered that our parents had once dated seriously. From then on we were determined to get them together, and — obviously — we succeeded.

At first, Mary Anne and I were ecstatic at the idea of becoming sisters. But things didn't fall into place quite as neatly as we'd planned.

Mary Anne and Richard came to live in our house, which was an adjustment for them.

Then, there was the food issue, which I've told you about. Mom didn't hit it off right away with Mary Anne's kitty, Tigger. Richard had to get used to Mom's messiness, and she had to get used to his neatness. But the thing that shocked me the most was that Mary Anne and I had to adjust to one another.

I'd thought we were so close that it would be a snap. It wasn't. In the beginning, we really got on each other's nerves. Living with someone is *not* the same as being friends with her.

Slowly, though, everything started to work out. Things improved a lot between Mary Anne and me once we had our own rooms instead of trying to sleep in the same one. And, little by little, each family member learned to make room for the others. We've been a pretty happy family for some time now. I suppose if anyone's been disrupting things it's me with my trips back and forth to California.

Jessi Ramsey and Mallory Pike slid into the room just as the digital clock turned to five-thirty. They're our junior members since they're eleven (the rest of us are thirteen) and are only allowed to baby-sit during the day unless they're sitting for members of their own families.

Jessi and Mallory are best friends. They're

both talented and a lot of fun. Yet, they're also very different from one another.

Mallory is the oldest of eight kids, which might explain why she's such a good baby-sitter. It could also explain why she wants to write and illustrate children's stories when she grows up. She's had a lot of experience making up stories for her younger brothers and sisters. One of her stories has already won an award in school. She's also written and directed a school play about what it's like to be part of a big family. One of the things I like best about Mal is her sense of humor. Sometimes she comes up with a snappy remark that just cracks me up.

Mal hates her looks, but I think she's cute. She has curly reddish-brown hair, brown eyes, and freckles. She can't stand her glasses, but I don't think they look bad on her. Someday she'll be able to get contact lenses if the glasses still annoy her. The clear braces she now wears — and despises — will also come off eventually. If you really study Mallory, you can tell she'll look just fine as she gets older.

And it isn't hard to see that Jessi is going to be a real beauty. She's already very pretty with her creamy, dark skin, large, brown eyes, and delicate features. She's tall with long legs and moves with incredible grace.

I don't know if Jessi became graceful

through years of ballet lessons, or she became a ballerina because she's naturally graceful. But, either way, she *is* a very gifted dancer. She's already been in several professional productions.

Jessi and her family moved into Stacey's old house during the time Stacey was back in New York City. Like Stacey, Jessi's father's company transferred him here. It was a big change for the Ramsey family, which consists of Jessi's mom and dad, her younger sister, Becca, her baby brother, Squirt, and her Aunt Cecelia, who helps out at home while Mrs. and Mr. Ramsey work. Not only did the family have to relocate (which can be hard enough by itself), but they were moving from an integrated neighborhood to an almost all-white one.

Some of their neighbors (the idiotic ones, if you ask me) got all upset about an African-American family moving in. Soon the bad feelings died down, though, and the Ramseys made some good friends in Stoneybrook.

Well, that's the BSC. Here's some quick club history.

Kristy came up with the idea for the club when she was in the seventh grade. One afternoon, she saw how difficult it was for her mother to find a baby-sitter for David Michael. Her mother was making lots of phone calls and having no luck. Kristy — who is always coming up with ideas — came up with a really brilliant one that day. She thought it would be great if her mother could call just one number and reach more than one baby-sitter.

Kristy told Mary Anne and Claudia that they should start a sitting business. Claudia suggested that Stacey join them. They decided to meet in Claudia's room every Monday, Wednesday, and Friday to be available to take baby-sitting jobs during that time. (Claudia has her own phone number, so they could take calls without disturbing anyone's family.)

They advertised in the paper and by putting up fliers around town. The phone started ringing quickly — and it hasn't stopped since.

In no time, the girls were so busy they needed another member. That was when Mary Anne suggested I join the club. Everything was going great for awhile until Stacey had to go back to New York City. That was when we invited Jessi and Mallory to join. By the time Stacey returned we were *so* busy that we needed her desperately.

That's how the BSC came to be. Here's how we work.

We still meet for half an hour three times a week. During that time clients call and the person nearest the phone answers. She writes down the job info and says we'll call right back. We decide who should take the job, call back, and that's that.

Sound simple? You'd think so. But it's not.

That's why we all (except Jessi and Mal because they're younger) have official titles and special jobs that go along with those titles.

Kristy is president since the club was her idea and she's so naturally presidential. Even though we don't always like her rules and regulations, they do hold things together.

It was her idea to keep track of every job assignment in a record book so there'd never be any confusion. The record book also contains our other nonbaby-sitting appointments as well as the names, phone numbers, allergies, special needs, and so forth of our clients.

It was also her idea to keep a club notebook in which we report on our most recent jobs. This is a big help if you need to know anything that's been happening with a family for whom you're going to sit. You can pick up a lot of helpful baby-sitting hints by reading through the notebook.

Another Kristy brainstorm was Kid-Kits. They're special boxes crammed with games, puzzles, books, crayons, glitter pens, pads, and whatever else we think would be fun for our sitting charges. We don't bring the Kid-Kits to every single job because we want them to remain a special treat. But if we are expecting a job to be difficult (for example, if the kid is sick or doesn't know us yet or is out of sorts for some reason), we bring our Kid-Kit along and it often saves the day.

Our vice-president is Claudia. She supplies snacks, and, of course, we use her room and phone. For those reasons, it seemed fair to make her vice-president.

Mary Anne has the hugely important job of secretary. She's the keeper of the club record book and she's an ace with it. She's the one who schedules sitting jobs, making sure everyone gets a fair turn.

Now that Stacey is back, she's once again club treasurer. Every week she collects dues which we use for things such as Claudia's phone bill and paying Charlie (Kristy's brother) to drive Shannon and Kristy to meetings. Dues also pay for some of the stuff that goes into our Kid-Kits. If anything is left over, we do something fun such as have a sleepover or pizza party.

The last official title is alternate officer. That's like being a permanent stand-in. The alternate officer must be ready to jump in and take over the job of anyone who might be absent. I started out as alternate officer, then Shannon took over. Now Shannon is an associate member again. She comes to meetings often, but doesn't have to come all the time.

No sooner had everyone settled down, when the phone started ringing. Mary Anne opened the club record book and we were soon busy figuring out who could take what work and when.

I leaned against the wall beside Claudia's bed and watched. Mallory and Jessi were discussing which one of them would rather take a sitting job the following afternoon. Mary Anne was checking their schedules. Claudia was on the phone, writing down the details of yet another assignment. Shannon was talking to Kristy about restocking her Kid-Kit, while Stacey checked the manila envelope where she kept the dues to see how much money we could afford to give Shannon for her kit.

It was wonderful to see everyone working together. The BSC is not only a club and a business, it's a close-knit family. How could I possibly leave?

I couldn't.

But I had to.

CHAPTER 3

The next Tuesday evening, I had to baby-sit for the Prezziosos. I returned home around eight. As soon as I walked into the house the phone rang. I knew Mary Anne was still out baby-sitting, but I assumed *someone* was home to pick it up. It kept ringing and ringing, so I dashed into the kitchen and snapped up the receiver. "Hello?"

"Hi, Dawn."

"Jeff!" I cried happily. It was so great to hear my brother's voice. In my mind I could see him, skinny and tanned, with spikey, sun-bleached hair and super-blue eyes. "What's happening?" I asked.

"Nothing much," said Jeff. "Just hanging out. What's happening with you?"

"Baby-sitting and hanging out," I said.

"I saw Sunny yesterday," Jeff reported.

"Oh, yeah? How did she . . . you know . . . seem?"

"All right. Why?"

"Well, I was worried since her mother is sick and all."

"Oh, right," said Jeff. "I didn't talk to her that much. She was with some guy who was giving her a surfing lesson."

Some guy? I couldn't imagine who it might have been. Why hadn't she mentioned him the other day?

"Dad wants to get on the phone," said Jeff.

In a moment my dad's voice came over the wire. "Hi, Sunshine," he said.

"Hi, Dad." Hearing his voice made me miss him so much.

He talked to me a little about his job and about some plans he had to retile the bathroom. "Things sure seem quiet here without you," he said.

I could feel a lump forming in my throat.

Then I heard a voice in the background. "Hi, hon!" I knew it was Carol, his new wife. When I first met Carol she rubbed me the wrong way. She tried too hard to be hip and perky. She got on my nerves. But I've grown to like her. I discovered that she really is loaded with energy (it's not fake perkiness) and down deep she's a sincere, genuine person.

"Want to say hi to Dawn?" Dad asked Carol.

"Sure." Carol got on the phone. "Hi, Dawn.

Guess what? I ran into Whitney Cater's mom, Annette, today. She asked how you are."

Whitney Cater is a girl I know in Palo City who has Down's syndrome. When I was in the We ♥ Kids Club her parents hired me to stay with her even though Whitney is twelve. Whitney and I became close. The We ♥ Kids Club even made her an honorary member and special helper. Whitney was yet another person I missed.

"Well?" said Carol expectantly.

"Well, what?" I asked.

"Well, how *are* you?" Carol laughed.

"I'm fine," I said, "except . . ." I glanced around the house. No one but me appeared to be home.

"Except what?"

"I really want to come back to Palo City and be with you guys," I whispered just in case anyone *was* around.

"Super!" Carol cried. "Come on back, then."

"I don't know," I continued whispering. "I have to talk to Mom. She might be pretty upset. And Mary Anne would really — " I cut myself short because I heard someone come in the front door. "I'll talk to you about this later," I told Carol. "Maybe I better go."

"All right, sweetheart. Can I tell your dad about this?"

"I guess so," I agreed. "We can talk more after I talk to Mom about it."

"Okay. 'Bye," Carol said as she hung up.

Mom appeared in the kitchen doorway. "Talk to me about what?" she asked.

Suddenly I felt cold all over. My heart pounded. It wasn't fear. Not exactly. It was more like a blend of nervousness and guilt. I knew Mom wasn't going to like what I was about to say. But I had to say it.

"Mom, can we talk about something?" I asked. "It's important."

Mom set the grocery bags she was carrying on the kitchen table. "Who was on the phone?"

"Jeff and Dad and Carol."

Mom pressed her lips together and a worried look came over her face. I wondered if she'd guessed what was going on.

She walked into the living room and I followed. We sat on the couch across from one another. "I'm listening," Mom began calmly.

My mouth went dry. This was incredibly hard to explain. I wasn't even sure where to begin. "Ever since I . . ." My voice was so raspy I stopped to clear my throat. "Lately, I've been thinking," I started again, then ran out of words.

Mom just sat and waited.

"All right," I said. "This is the thing . . ."

"Dawn, honey, just come out with it," Mom said.

I shut my eyes and balled my hands into fists. "I want to move back to California."

I opened my eyes and saw that Mom looked slightly pale although her expression was blank. "For how long?" she asked after a moment.

"To stay," I replied in a small voice.

Mom turned white and leaned back hard against the couch. For a moment, I was worried that she might faint. Slowly, though, spots of pink returned to her cheeks and forehead. "Dawn, why?" she asked.

I clenched my hands together. How could I explain this? "You grew up here in Stoneybrook, so this feels like home to you. But I grew up in Palo City. I mean, there are a lot of great things about Stoneybrook, but Palo City is home to me. There are so many things I miss there."

"Like Dad and Jeff," Mom filled in quietly.

"Yeah. And I miss Sunny and my other friends. I miss being near the beach and going to school at Vista and the kids I baby-sat for out there."

"What about the BSC, and your friends here, and the kids you sit for here?" Mom asked. "Won't you miss them?"

"Sure," I said. "But I've lived in Palo City

a lot longer than I've lived here."

Mom leaned forward and put her hands over mine. "Dawn, is something wrong? Is there something going on in the family you want to talk about?"

"No, Mom, honest, everything is fine here."

Mom's eyes glistened. "Then why?" she asked, tossing out her hands in frustration. "Why do you want to go? I don't understand."

"Mom, I love you," I said as the tears spilled over and ran down my cheeks. "I just think I'd be happier in Palo City."

As I spoke I felt a pang in my chest, as if admitting out loud that I wanted to leave was causing an actual pain. Tears fell from my eyes now.

Mom moved closer and wrapped her arm around me. "Are you sure about this?" she asked softly.

I nodded my head as I wiped away tears.

At this point, Richard came home. "What's the matter?" he asked, putting down his briefcase.

Mom looked up at him and forced a small smile. "Dawn has decided she might be happier living in California permanently," she said in a quiet, controlled voice.

Looking stunned, Richard sat down in the armchair across from the couch. "Is something the matter with living here?" he asked.

"It's not that she *doesn't* like it here," Mom said. "It's that she misses a lot about California."

Richard took a deep breath. "How do you feel about it, Sharon?" he asked Mom.

"I hate it," said Mom with a sob as she squeezed my hands. "But this is Dawn's decision. How can I say no if that's what she really wants to do?"

I threw my arms around Mom. "You know I'll always call and I'll come back for long visits," I said through my tears.

Mom held me tight and I could tell from the way her body was shaking that she was crying now, too. After a few moments more she let me go and brushed some wet strands of hair from my face.

"I love you, Mom," I said again. "I really do."

"I know," she replied. "And you know I love you, too."

"Does your father know about this change of plans yet?" Richard asked.

"Probably," I answered. "I mentioned it to Carol just now. She's probably told him."

"New custody papers will have to be drawn up," he said. Since Richard is a lawyer, he thinks of these things right away.

"We'll have to call your dad," said Mom. "You'll have to clear it with him."

"I don't think he'll mind," I said.

Mom shook her head as she stood up from the couch. "No, I'm sure he won't. Let me go call him now." She had almost reached the kitchen when she stopped and turned back to me. "Does Mary Anne know about this?" she asked.

I shook my head.

Telling Mom was upsetting enough. The thought of breaking the news to Mary Anne was almost unbearable.

CHAPTER 4

Wednesday

I can't believe I thought yesterday was just going to be a boring day baby-sitting for my sisters and brother. I never ever expected such a dull day to end in disaster. But I guess no one ever does expect that, do they?

At our Wednesday meeting Mallory spent almost the entire half hour writing in the club notebook about what had happened to her on Tuesday when she took her sisters and brother to the Hobarts'. It was some story!

Mrs. Pike sometimes works as a secretary. She only goes into the office when the temporary agency she's signed up with calls her. Yesterday they had a job for her, which meant Mallory had to sit for Margo, who is seven; Nicky, who is eight; and Claire, who is five. (Vanessa, who's nine, and the ten-year-old triplets, Adam, Byron, and Jordan, had been invited to a friend's pool.)

Even though the kids were behaving, Mal was bored. (I suppose if they hadn't been good she would have been aggravated instead of bored. Not much of a choice.) Baby-sitting for your own siblings couldn't possibly be as much fun as baby-sitting for other kids since you see your siblings all the time.

Mal decided to call her friend Ben Hobart. Actually, I'm not sure whether to refer to him as her friend or her boyfriend. They don't go out on dates and I've never seen them even hold hands. But they've gone to school dances together and on an occasional trip to the movies.

Ben is in the sixth grade with Mal and Jessi. He's tall with reddish blond hair, freckles, and glasses, and has the cutest Australian accent. (He and his family moved from Australia into Mary Anne's old house on Bradford Court after Mary Anne and Richard came to live with Mom and me.)

"What are you up to?" Mallory asked Ben when she called.

"Nothing much," he replied. "Baby-sitting." Ben has three younger brothers, James (eight), Mathew (six), and Johnny (four). Ben's brothers look just like him, although they don't wear glasses.

"Too bad," Mal said with a sigh. "If we weren't both stuck at home maybe we could go to the pool or something."

"I know what we could do together," said Ben brightly.

"What?"

"Baby-sit!"

"Cool," said Mallory. "Do you want to bring your brothers here, or should we come to your place?"

"I don't care. Come here," Ben suggested.

"Great. I'm dying to get out of the house. We'll be right over."

She hung up and called down the stairs to the kids who were in the rec room. "Hey, guys! Come on up!"

Nicky and Vanessa thundered up the stairs. Mal had to wait longer for Claire to arrive

39

carrying their pet hamster, Frodo. "Why isn't he in his cage?" Mallory asked.

"He was lonely," Claire replied.

"Go put him back and then get your sneakers. We're going over to the Hobarts'."

This news was greeted with cheers. The Pike kids liked the Hobarts and they were probably bored, too.

At the Hobarts' house Ben greeted them at the door.

"Claire! Claire!" cried Johnny. "Come see my new iguanas!"

Mallory wrinkled her nose and looked at Ben. "Iguanas?"

"They're small ones," he assured her.

Claire and Johnny hurried up the stairs.

"Hey, Nicky. Margo. We were just about to go outside and play a game of football," said James, entering the living room with Mathew. "Want to play with us?"

"How could the two of you play football by yourselves?" Margo asked, puzzled. "Were you just going to toss the ball back and forth?"

"You mean kick it back and forth," Mathew corrected her.

A bewildered expression crossed Margo's face. "I know you kick it in the beginning but . . ."

"I remember!" Nicky cried. "In Australia they call soccer football."

40

"Why?" Margo asked.

"It makes sense," said Ben. "In soccer what do you use to move the ball?"

"Your feet, mostly," Margo replied.

"Well?" said Ben. "Foot. Ball."

"I suppose," Margo agreed.

"It's stupid, if you ask me," said Nicky.

"Nobody asked you," Mallory pointed out drily.

"Why is it stupid?" Ben asked.

"Because soccer is soccer and football is football."

"What's stupid is the way Americans play football," said Mallory firmly. "I don't see the point in all these people crashing into one another just for fun. How could that possibly be fun?"

"It sounds like fun to me," James spoke up.

"Want me to teach you?" Nicky offered.

"Yeah!" James and Mathew cried.

"No," said Margo. "I don't want to play that."

"Okay, you stay in here with Mallory and Ben," Nicky told her. "Besides, girls are dweebs at *real* football."

"Are not!" Margo shot back angrily.

Nicky held up his pinky finger and began dancing around the room. "Oh, I bent my little finger! Ouch! Ouch! Ouch!" he sang in a high, whiney voice.

Margo swatted him on the arm. "I'm not like that, and I'll prove it. Come on!"

With Margo in the lead, the kids headed out to the backyard. "She's actually not a bad football player," Mallory commented to Ben. "She's fast."

"I'm not really that big on American football," said Ben.

"That shows intelligence."

"My mom made a chocolate cake. Want some?" Ben offered.

"Yeah, thanks!"

Mallory and Ben went into the kitchen and Ben cut them each a slice of cake, which they took to the table. "This was a great idea," Mallory told Ben.

"What? The cake?"

"The cake is awesome, but I meant having us over. The kids are happier and we can hang out."

Mallory checked out the kitchen window and could see James, Mathew, Margo, and Nicky racing back and forth, shouting and laughing.

Nicky tossed James's soccer ball through the air in a long, smooth arch as if it were an American-style football. James caught the ball and was instantly jumped on by Margo, Mathew, and then Nicky.

"One of them is going to get hurt," Mallory

said, worried, as she broke off a forkful of cake.

"They'll be fine." Ben got a carton of milk from the refrigerator. "I think my brothers are made of rubber."

Mallory wasn't as sure. Margo certainly wasn't made of rubber, and Nicky wasn't nearly as tough as he thought. She kept glancing anxiously out the window.

In a few minutes, Claire and Johnny came into the kitchen, having grown tired of the iguanas. "Would you turn the sprinkler on for us?" said Johnny.

"Do you mind if Claire gets wet?" Ben asked Mallory.

"No, it's hot," she replied as she brought the plates to the sink. Ben cleared away their glasses and then they took Claire and Johnny out to the yard.

As soon as they reached the yard they saw James fall down as Nicky and Mathew leapt fiercely on top of him. Margo threw herself onto all three of them and rolled right over them, landing on her back with a thud.

"Are you okay?" Mallory cried, running to Margo.

Margo looked up at her and blinked hard. In a gasping, raspy voice she managed to eke out the words, "I can't talk."

"She's had the wind knocked out of her,"

said Ben, kneeling beside Mallory. "Get up slowly, Margo."

He helped Margo sit forward. She wrapped her arms around her knees and took short breaths. "I feel better now," she said in a small, croaking voice.

An awful, pain-filled moan made Mallory whirl around sharply. Behind her, James writhed on the grass clutching his leg.

Ben rolled his eyes. "He's so dramatic," he said.

Mal was on her feet quickly. "No, Ben. He's really hurt. I think he's hurt badly."

James let go of his leg and leaned back on his elbows. He scrunched up his face, trying to control the pain.

Mallory gasped at the sight of his leg. It was bent at an angle she never would have believed possible. "It's broken," she cried.

"What do we do?" Ben asked.

"I'll call nine-one-one. Or maybe I should just call an ambulance," Mallory said frantically.

"The numbers for police, fire, and ambulance are by the phone," Ben told her.

Mallory raced into the kitchen and called the ambulance. "Hello, this is Mallory Pike. I'm baby-sitting and one of the kids just broke his leg. It looks pretty bad."

The dispatcher asked Mallory a few questions about James's condition, then took down the address. "Don't touch him. The ambulance will be there right away," she advised Mallory.

Mal ran back into the yard. "They're coming," she said breathlessly. "Don't touch him."

She knelt beside James, whose face was now bright red. She took hold of his hand and squeezed. "It'll be all right," she told him, wishing she could come up with something more helpful to say.

James just wrinkled his face in pain, keeping his eyes shut tightly. Mal felt terrible for him.

"Should I get a wet cloth for his forehead?" Margo offered.

"Good idea," said Mallory. In truth she knew a wet cloth wouldn't do much good but it was better than just sitting there, waiting.

Margo and Mathew ran inside for the cloth. Johnny started crying. And Claire put her arm around Johnny comfortingly.

Margo returned with the wet cloth that Ben used to mop James's bruised, dirty forehead.

In only ten minutes (which Mal said felt like ten years) they heard the whooping siren of the ambulance as it approached. From the sound, they knew when it pulled to a stop in front of the house. Ben ran to the front and quickly returned with two medics, a man and a woman in white coats carrying a stretcher.

With amazing efficiency, they lifted James onto the stretcher. Mal, Ben, and the kids followed them back to the ambulance.

Alerted by the siren, neighbors had run from their houses to see what was happening. Claudia rushed across the street. "Who's sick?" she asked Mallory.

"James broke his leg."

"Oh, my gosh!" Claudia gasped.

"Mallory," Ben said. "I have to go to the hospital with James. Could you stay and babysit for Johnny and Mathew?"

"Sure," Mallory replied. "Where can I call your parents?"

"The number's on the fridge. Thanks." Ben hopped into the back of the ambulance and the medic shut the door. Once again the siren screamed as the ambulance zoomed from the curb.

"Poor kid," Claudia murmured.

Claud and Mal took the kids inside and settled them in the living room where they watched a video. Mallory called one of the two numbers written on a paper under a magnet on the refrigerator. The first was a work number for Mr. Hobart, but he was out of the office. The second was a soup kitchen where Mrs. Hobart volunteered, but no one was sure where she was. Mallory left messages at both places for the Hobarts to go to the emergency room of the hospital right away.

By five o'clock Mallory still hadn't heard from anyone. She called home to tell her mother, who was back from work, what was going on. "Bring all the kids over here," Mrs. Pike suggested.

"All right," Mal agreed. "But I want to hang out for another hour in case Ben or his parents call here."

By five-thirty no one had called. Just when Mal thought the waiting would drive her crazy, the phone rang.

It was Ben.

"Mom and Dad are here," he told her. "They got your messages and came right down." He told her what was happening at the hospital and then said good-bye.

"Come on, kids," Mal called. "We're going to my house."

"How's James?" asked Claudia.

"He broke his leg in *two* places," Mallory told her.

Claudia grimaced.

"He had to have *surgery* to put pins into his leg," Mallory added.

"But he'll be all right, won't he?" asked Claudia.

Mallory nodded. "I guess so. But I sure feel sorry for him. Just think, a big cast on your leg in the middle of summer vacation."

CHAPTER 5

On Wednesday, Mary Anne had been busy running between a daytime baby-sitting job, the meeting, and another sitting job in the evening. If she hadn't been so busy, she would have picked up on the fact that *something* was going on at our house.

For one thing, Mom was much quieter than usual and she was on the phone a lot with Dad. Richard sat in the living room and reviewed the existing custody agreement while he made notes on a long yellow legal pad.

But Mary Anne was out and I was relieved. If she'd been home, I would have had to come up with a way to tell her what was going on.

How could I explain it to her? No matter what I said I knew she'd see it only one way. To her it would seem as if I were leaving because I didn't care about her.

Mary Anne is the most sensitive person I've ever met. She cries very easily. If she even hears about something bad happening to someone, she gets upset.

Her kindness and loyalty are wonderful. But Mary Anne's sensitivity also causes her to feel hurt deeply when someone she cares about disappoints her.

And I was about to disappoint her — big time.

Mary Anne was going to take this personally. I knew her too well to hope even for a moment that she wouldn't.

The only thing I could do was try to come up with the kindest, gentlest, most understandable way of explaining it. And the more I thought about it, the more impossible it seemed.

By Thursday afternoon, I'd practically worn myself out trying to come up with a way to tell her. What could I possibly say? *Mary Anne, you and I have been incredibly close both as friends and sisters, but now I prefer my family and friends on the other side of the country. So, 'bye.* I could easily imagine the stunned, hurt look on her face. I couldn't hurt Mary Anne like that. I just couldn't.

Mary Anne was out with Logan somewhere that afternoon, so I had some time to think about what to say before she came home. By the evening, though, I was determined to come up with something.

I sat on the living room couch and thought until I had a headache. I needed a break. Perhaps if I gave my mind a rest, the perfect explanation — one that would make sense to Mary Anne — would simply come to me. My mind works that way sometimes.

I took a notepad and pen from the kitchen junk drawer, went out to the backyard, and settled in on the lounge chair. I was going to put Mary Anne out of my mind for the moment and make a list of the things I needed to do before I left for California.

First, I wrote an obvious one. Pack.

The second thing was to ask Mom to have my grade transcripts sent from SMS to my school in California.

For number three, I wrote *BSC stuff.* What did I have to do there? I considered.

Suddenly, I sat forward in the chair. I realized there were only a few more weeks before school started again. The beginning of school is a very busy time because people would be home from vacation and kids back from camp. Kristy would have a fit if she was short one sitter right then.

The sooner I told Kristy what I was going to do, the better it would be for the club. She's very choosy when it comes to letting new people join the club. It's not that she's snobby, but she insists on only letting in members who will be responsible and cooperative.

When I left for California the first time, Kristy had a bad experience when she tried to replace me. The new girl couldn't be counted on to come to meetings or to show up on time for jobs. That made Kristy even more particular about whom she wants in the club.

The most responsible thing I could do was give her plenty of time to find a replacement she could train properly. Kristy would want to put her through a trial period. In order to do it the right way, Kristy needed as much time as possible.

I had to tell her right away. Of course, she wouldn't like the news, but it would be easier than telling Mary Anne.

I ran into the house and punched in Kristy's number. "Hi, what's up?" she asked cheerfully when she answered the phone.

"Uhhhh," I hesitated. "Well . . . this is the thing."

"What?" Kristy asked, sounding concerned.

"I've decided that what would really make me happy is . . . is . . . to move back to California."

There was silence on the other end.

"Kristy?" I asked after a moment. "Are you there?"

"Do you mean you're leaving for good?"

"Yeah."

"Oh, no! Why?"

I ran through my reasons — how I'd lived there longer than I'd lived here and my last trip back made me realize how much I missed the place and the people there. I pointed out that I'd be back a lot for visits so it wasn't that I was disappearing or anything.

"But you can't be a BSC member in California," Kristy said.

"No," I agreed. "I can't."

Kristy sighed long and deep. "Are you sure about this?"

"I think so."

"That doesn't sound very certain to me. Maybe you should think about it some more."

I couldn't believe how difficult she was making this! "I have thought about it," I told her. "And I'm sure it's what I need to do. You're the first one of my friends I've told because I figured you'd want to start thinking about replacing me in the club."

"Mary Anne knows, though, doesn't she?"

"Not yet," I admitted sheepishly.

"Are you kidding?" Kristy cried. "When are you going to tell her?"

"When I get up the nerve."

"Good luck," said Kristy.

"I'm not looking forward to it. Listen, though, you've got to keep this top secret. All right? Don't tell anyone before I break the news to Mary Anne."

"Sure," said Kristy. "I understand. I'm really bummed about this, Dawn. I'm going to miss you. It was different before, when I knew you were coming back. This is good-bye for good."

"No, it's not. I *will* be back," I reminded her. "My parents are going over the custody arrangements. I'll probably be back for the summers and definitely for some holidays."

"That's true," said Kristy. "Um, thanks for telling me anyway, I guess," she said. "I'll see you tomorrow."

"Right. See you tomorrow." I hung up. My emotions were all mixed together. One of my feelings was relief. I'd survived breaking the news to Kristy. It hadn't been *that* bad.

Another of my feelings was sadness. Telling Kristy to start looking for my replacement made my decision to leave seem very real. It was as if, one by one, I was closing the doors on my life here in Stoneybrook — closing and locking them.

When I'd left the first time I had told everyone: "I'll be back! I promise! I'll be back. Hold a space for me. Don't change anything."

Now I was going to tell everyone to fill in the space where I'd been. Telling Kristy was just the first step.

That evening, Mary Anne dashed in, ate dinner, then ran out again to sit for the Prezziosos. It gave me another evening to sit and think about what to tell her.

Around ten that evening Mary Anne came into my room. I was lying on my bed thumbing through a magazine, not really paying attention to it. "Hi," she said, perching on the edge of my bed.

"Hi," I replied as I shut the magazine.

"I just came in to see how you were doing. I feel like I haven't even talked to you for awhile."

"I'm okay."

"I've been running around like a nut these last couple of days. I've taken so many babysitting jobs, and Logan is on this kick that the summer will end soon so we should do as many fun things as possible while we still can."

"That sounds like a pretty good idea."

"I know," Mary Anne said, smiling. "We went biking today. But I hope you don't feel that I've been . . . you know . . . ignoring you or anything like that."

That was Mary Anne for you, always thinking about the other person's feelings.

I smiled at her. "No. I'm all right. But thanks for asking."

"Are you sure?"

"Sure."

Mary Anne studied me closely. She was probably trying to figure out if I was being sincere. "Logan wanted to go to the movies tomorrow night, but I'll tell him no," she said. "You and I are going to spend the evening together. We'll figure out something to do. I know! I'd like to make a pizza. We could put healthy stuff on it, but not tofu. We could even rent a video to watch while it's cooking."

"That's nice, Mary Anne, but you don't have to do that," I told her. If she went to the movies with Logan, it would give me another evening to figure out how to tell her my news.

Mary Anne got off the bed. "No, it'll be fun, don't you think?"

"It would be great, but . . ."

"Then that's what we'll do. I've missed spending time with you, Dawn. I have. So, I'll get the pizza stuff we need. Then after the BSC meeting we can go to the video store together. Okay?"

Mary Anne's plan did sound like fun. After all, who knew how many more evenings we'd get to spend together.

"Sure," I said with a smile. Maybe I could tell her tomorrow. We'd be alone together. She'd be in a good mood.

Or so I thought.

CHAPTER 6

By early Friday afternoon, I knew what I would say to Mary Anne. I even wrote it down on an index card. *Mary Anne, you are one of the most important people in my entire life. You've been a wonderful friend. The best friend anyone could want. And before I met you, I always wanted a sister. In my wildest dreams I couldn't have imagined a better sister than you. Because we're so close — and always will be — I know you're going to understand what I'm about to say.*

Then I would tell her what was going on and how I was feeling. I'd finish by saying: *Nothing will ever ever change the way I feel about you. I'll write you all the time and call as much as I can. I'll be back for visits and you can come visit me. It won't be that bad. I know we'll always be together, sisters and friends forever.*

It sounded pretty good to me and I meant every word of it. Now, I prayed Mary Anne would believe it, too.

"Hi!" she called from the front door as she came inside with her arms wrapped around two brown grocery bags. "I got all the stuff we need for the pizza."

I ran to take a bag from her. "I'll pay you for half of this," I offered.

"It's okay. I'm feeling rich since I've been baby-sitting so much. It's my treat."

We set the bags down in the kitchen, then argued agreeably for a few minutes about who would pay. She finally agreed to let me give her some money toward the pizza. "I found this great frozen premade pizza dough," she said, unpacking it from the bag. "I didn't know if it would be okay for you, since I think it must have preservatives. But I bought it anyway and figured if you didn't like it we could just — "

Mary Anne was interrupted by the ringing of the phone. "Hello?" she said, picking it up. "Oh, hi, Logan."

I pulled things out of the bag and put them on the table while she listened to Logan.

"What news?" Mary Anne asked, sounding puzzled.

I looked at her, wondering what Logan's news was myself. Her face grew pale as her brows dipped into a frown.

What could Logan be telling her?

"Who told you that?" Mary Anne spoke into

the phone in an agitated voice. "Well, how would Robert know?"

When I heard the name Robert, I became even more curious. Remember, I told you Robert is Stacey's boyfriend? It had to be some news about Stacey.

Suddenly feeling worried, I stopped unpacking and sat on a chair. "This is unbelievable," Mary Anne murmured. "I just can't . . . I . . ."

I was bursting to know what he was saying. "What?" I asked Mary Anne, but she ignored me.

"Thanks for calling," Mary Anne said quietly. " 'Bye." She hung up and turned toward me. Her expression was distant, as if she'd heard something so terrible that she couldn't quite take it in.

"What happened?" I asked anxiously.

"That was Logan."

"I know. What did he say?"

The dazed look melted away from Mary Anne's eyes and was replaced by sparks of anger. "He was calling to find out how I was taking the news about your moving back to California," she said furiously.

It was my turn to be stunned. "Robert told him that?" I gulped.

Mary Anne nodded. "Apparently, you told Kristy, who told Claudia, who told Stacey, who told Robert, who told Logan, who just told me!"

Never in my entire life had I wished to disappear more than I did at that moment.

"Is it true?" Mary Anne asked me, her voice filled with quiet anger.

I nodded.

Then Mary Anne did something so shocking and out of her character that I couldn't believe my eyes. She picked up a used coffee cup that had been left on the counter and deliberately smashed it on the kitchen floor.

Crash! The ceramic pieces shattered.

I jumped to my feet in surprise.

"How could you, Dawn? How could you?" she yelled, sobbing.

"I was going to tell you today . . . tonight!" I defended myself. "When we were making pizza."

Tears welled up in Mary Anne's eyes, but she didn't crumble. She remained standing, her fists clenched. "Why? Why are you going?"

"I have to, Mary Anne," I began. All the words I'd written flew out of my head. It seemed idiotic to look at index cards now. "I miss Palo City. It's my home."

"*This* is your home!"

"No, Mary Anne. Stoneybrook is *your* home."

"What a jerk I am," Mary Anne said bitterly. "I thought we were a family. I thought you and I were sisters. All the time you were in California this year I told myself to trust you. That you'd be back because you said you would be. Ha! What a joke."

"I did come back," I insisted.

"Oh, yeah, you came back — to get your things."

"I came back to stay. I couldn't predict how I was going to feel."

"Oh, too bad," said Mary Anne scornfully, turning her back on me. "You couldn't predict that we wouldn't be cool enough for you after your fabulous time in California. Sorry we're so boring now. Sorry I'm such a drag compared to everyone in California."

"Mary Anne, it's not like that at all!"

"Oh, then what is it like? Is it like I was fun for awhile but now you've moved on to the next thing?"

"No!"

"Yes, that's exactly what it is. Dawn, you're so selfish. All you care about is what *you* want. What about how your mother feels? What about the BSC? What about me? None of that counts, I guess. All that counts are your feelings. Your selfish, selfish feelings."

"Cut it out, Mary Anne," I said quietly. "I have a right to do what makes me happy. I have a perfect right to be happy! You don't live my life. I do. You're totally happy here so you think I have to be. Talk about selfish. You're the selfish one."

"*Me?*" Mary Anne cried.

"Yes, you! You act like you're just poor, sweet Mary Anne who wouldn't hurt a fly. You're never to blame for anything. That's because you never *do* anything! You just react to what's happening around you, you never act. You never start anything. Well, I'm not you. I act! And if you want to blame me for not being you, go ahead, but I'll never be you, and I'm glad!"

Mary Anne whirled around and faced me. I could see that my words had shocked her. They'd shocked even me.

But now I was mad, too. Furious.

We stood facing each other, out of breath.

Slowly, Mary Anne regained control of herself. Her breathing slowed and she wiped the tears from her eyes. The crimson color on her cheeks subsided to pink.

"I never knew you felt that way about me," Mary Anne said coolly. "But now that I do know, it's probably for the best that you're leaving."

Her words left me nearly breathless. Had I meant to say those things? Maybe part of me had, but that wasn't really how I felt.

"Mary Anne, I . . . I . . . didn't mean exactly that . . ." I started to stammer. "You know how I really . . ."

"Yes, I do know exactly how you feel," she said in a cold voice. "Because I was the last person to find out about this."

"Mary Anne!" I cried helplessly.

"Don't worry about it," she said as she headed out of the kitchen. "I still have my other friends, and I have Logan. I'll be fine."

When she'd left, I stood gazing at the spot where she'd been. The unopened pizza ingredients still sat on the table. Hot tears burned in my eyes. I scrunched my face up, but they spilled over anyway. There was a terrible, hollow feeling in the pit of my stomach. I felt as if I'd done something awful — something which could never be undone.

No matter what Mary Anne and I said to one another from now on, nothing would ever be the same between us again.

I sat down heavily in the chair. Resting my hands on my arms, I began to sob.

That afternoon, as I approached Claudia's house for our Friday BSC meeting, I was in a pretty horrible mood. Not only did I feel terrible about my fight with Mary Anne, but I was angry with my friends for having such big mouths — especially Kristy.

Mary Anne had gone on ahead, which didn't surprise me. I climbed the steps to Claudia's room and heard her voice. "It's not your fault, Kristy."

"Yes, it is," Kristy replied glumly.

"Not entirely," I heard Shannon say.

When I stepped into the room, Kristy, Stacey, Claudia, Shannon, and Mary Anne all looked at me.

Kristy sat forward in the director's chair and pushed up the brim of the green visor she often wore during meetings. "Hi, Dawn. I'm really, really sorry about telling Claudia," she said.

Claudia sat on her bed with her arms folded and looked at me guiltily.

"She was *supposed* to keep quiet about it," added Kristy, scowling at Claudia.

"I thought Stacey would keep quiet. How was I supposed to know she'd go tell Robert?" Claudia mumbled with a sidelong glance at Stacey, who was sitting on the other end of the bed.

"I'll kill Robert," said Stacey to me. "Honest, I didn't expect him to shoot off his mouth to Logan."

"None of this would have happened if Kristy had just kept *her* mouth shut like she promised," I said.

"None of this would have happened if you'd just told me how you were feeling," Mary Anne countered.

I sighed. In a way, she was right. I still felt annoyed with my friends. But I was as much to blame as they were. I should have talked to Mary Anne instead of trying to guess how she was going to feel.

"Mary Anne, the only reason I didn't tell you right away was because I was trying to think of the perfect words to explain why I was going," I said, trying to explain.

At that moment, Mallory came into the room with Jessi behind her. "Who's going? Where?" she asked.

"Dawn has decided to move to California for good," Claudia told her.

"Really?" cried Jessi.

"I'll miss everyone, but I think it's where I'll be happiest," I said quietly. I was still very aware of Mary Anne's feelings and didn't want to say anything to make her feel even worse. I'd stopped being mad about what she'd said during our argument. She had every right to be upset and I knew it.

Mallory sat down, cross-legged, in her usual spot on the floor. "It's important to be happy," she observed.

"It's what we all want," agreed Jessi, sitting beside her. "For you to be happy."

I appreciated their understanding.

"When are you leaving?" asked Stacey.

"I'm not sure," I replied. "Mom talked to my dad last night and they decided I should be there in time to get settled and start school, which begins a week earlier than SMS. So, I guess I'll have to leave in two weeks."

Mary Anne looked at me sharply, surprise in her eyes, but she didn't say anything. I knew how she felt. Everything was happening fast.

"Two weeks," Mallory said. "That's so soon."

"I know. But I want you guys to know that I'm going to be visiting a lot. I'll be back for at least part of every summer and on holidays. So, this isn't good-bye forever or anything like that."

I checked Mary Anne's response, but she had begun looking through the record book.

"Still, it won't be the same without you," said Claudia.

"I know what we should do," said Kristy. "We'll give Dawn a big going-away party."

"Great idea!" cried Mallory.

"You guys don't have to do that," I said, although I appreciated the idea.

"Sure we do," said Claudia. "We want to. Where should we have it?"

Mary Anne looked up from the record book. "We could use our barn," she suggested half-heartedly.

"Really?" asked Kristy. "Well, the weather will still be warm. That's a great idea!"

Despite Mary Anne's lack of enthusiasm, I was glad she'd made the suggestion. It showed she didn't hate me completely.

"At this meeting I was going to mention that we have a little money left over in the budget," said Stacey. "We could use it for the party."

"Excellent!" said Kristy.

The phone rang. It was Dr. Johanssen looking for someone to baby-sit for Charlotte the next Wednesday. Mary Anne checked the record book. "Stacey and Dawn are free," she reported after a moment. "But I suppose I shouldn't schedule any more jobs for Dawn."

"Probably not," I agreed. Surprisingly, it hurt to say that. It felt like yet another door shutting and locking behind me.

"I'll take it," Stacey said. "I'll be glad to see Char. I haven't seen her in awhile."

After we called back Dr. Johanssen, Kristy asked, "When should we have the party?"

"Not this week but next week." Shannon suggested.

"A week from Thursday. That sounds good to me," said Kristy.

Everyone agreed. That would leave just enough time to send out invitations and set things up. As the discussion continued I realized I was very happy about the party. It meant they didn't all feel betrayed by my leaving.

Only Mary Anne didn't get caught up in the excitement of planning the party. She just grew more and more quiet. I guess she had a lot to sort out.

The phone rang again. This time it was Mrs. Newton needing a sitter for Jamie and Lucy on Sunday night. Claudia called her back and said she could take the job.

"By the way, Mal," said Claudia after she had finished talking to Mrs. Newton. "How is James Hobart doing?"

"I talked to Ben today," said Mallory. "James will be all right. But right now he's not supposed to move around much and that's like torture for him. Ben says he's being really good about it, though."

"Poor kid," said Jessi sympathically.

Mallory shuddered. "I never saw a leg look like that. It was horrible. Nicky is such a maniac. He *had* to go teach them American football. And, all the while, I was worried that Margo would get creamed."

"It wasn't really Margo or Nicky's fault," said Jessi.

"I guess not. But they feel bad. They're trying to think of ways to cheer up James. So far, they haven't come up with anything."

"I wonder what they could do." Kristy began to muse.

"They could bake him something," Shannon suggested.

"No," said Mallory. "Mrs. Hobart bakes all the time, and she doesn't even use a mix. I'm sure that whatever Margo and Nicky baked would be totally gross compared to what James is used to."

"What about if they decorated his room?" said Claudia.

"They could make him cards," said Jessi.

Stacey laughed. "Baking, decorating, cards

— it's starting to sound like Christmas. Too bad it's still summertime."

"That's it!" Kristy cried.

"What's it?" asked Stacey.

"Christmas in summer. That's what we can do to cheer James up. Christmas is the most cheerful time of year, and the silliness of having it in summer is sure to cheer him up."

"But Margo and Nicky wanted to do something," Mallory reminded Kristy.

"They can help," said Kristy. "This is something a lot of the kids we sit for can help with. Half of them are bored silly by the end of the summer, anyway. They'd love this. We can make Christmas decorations and holiday food. We could even buy small gifts and wrap them in Christmas paper, and then surprise James one day by bringing Christmas right to him."

Jessi laughed. "What a great idea!"

"James will love it," Mallory agreed.

"*I* love it!" said Claudia. "I can't wait to get started."

"It *is* a good idea," I said.

"Will you have time to help?" Kristy asked me.

"I'll make time," I said. This would be the last project I'd be involved with as an official BSC member. I wasn't going to let that door shut — at least not yet.

CHAPTER 8

When Kristy gets a great, hot, new idea, she never waits around for it to grow cold. And now, she had two ideas to work on — Christmas in summer and my going-away party. The very next day, Saturday, she called a special planning meeting to get them both in gear.

The meeting was held in our barn, the one with the secret passage to my room. Just for fun, everyone met at the house and went to the barn through the passage.

"This special meeting will come to order," Kristy announced at one o'clock sharp. We sat in a circle on the dusty wood floor. Mary Anne had baked some chocolate chip cookies, which we passed around. She'd also sliced up apples for Stacey and me.

In the morning, while she was making the cookies, I'd come into the kitchen and offered to help. "No, thanks," she told me without

70

looking up from the chips she was pouring into a measuring cup. "I have it under control." She spoke in the same completely neutral, expressionless voice in which she'd talked to me since our fight Friday afternoon.

She wasn't exactly giving me the cold shoulder, but she wasn't being particularly nice, either. It was as if I'd hurt her so deeply that any feelings she had toward me — both the positive and the negative ones — had disappeared. It was weird.

"The first thing we should do is make up a guest list," said Kristy. "Mary Anne, since you're secretary, you write it down. Okay?"

"All right. I brought a pen and pad," Mary Anne replied.

"Are we inviting kids?" asked Mallory.

"What do you think, Dawn?" Kristy asked. "It's your party."

"Well, we could."

"No," Stacey disagreed. "If we invite kids we'll have to look after them and it will be more like a big baby-sitting job than a party."

"I agree," said Claudia, taking two cookies from the plate. "No kids."

"There are eight of us," said Mary Anne. "Nine including Logan. Who else?"

"Robert," said Stacey.

"Ben," added Mallory.

"Bart," said Kristy, mentioning a boy she

likes a lot, who is sort of her boyfriend.

"That's twelve," said Mary Anne.

"What about Emily Bernstein?" Claudia suggested. Emily is the editor of the school newspaper.

"Definitely," I said. I like Emily a lot.

We kept naming names until we were up to twenty guests. "I think that's enough," said Kristy. I agreed.

After that, we discussed what to serve at the party. "I suppose it will have to be healthy." Mary Anne sighed.

I was about to suggest pizza, but didn't. Mary Anne and I never did make our pizza and I was reluctant even to bring up the subject. "We could have some veggie, healthy stuff and some not," I said instead. "The way we always do it."

Claudia and Mallory agreed to be in charge of decorations. Kristy and Mary Anne would get the invitations out. Shannon and Jessi said they'd coordinate refreshments. Stacey volunteered to take charge of music. "What should I do?" I asked.

"Nothing. You're the guest of honor," Kristy said. "Technically, you shouldn't even be here, but we needed to know whom you'd like invited."

From there, the meeting progressed to planning our Christmas in summer. "It seems to me," said Kristy, "that we'll never get this together if we do it one activity at a time. We need to get the kids together in groups and do it all at once."

"Like Santa's summer workshop," said Jessi.

"Good idea," said Claudia. "Why don't we do it right here? This is a big enough space."

"That would be okay," said Mary Anne.

"Let's take the committee approach again," said Kristy. "One group can meet in here to make decorations. A second group will bake in the house. A third group of kids and sitters can go into town to shop for James's gifts. How does that sound?"

"It sounds fine," said Stacey, "but expensive. We have *some* extra in the treasury, enough for the party *or* Christmas in summer. There's not enough here to cover both, though."

"Hmmmm." Kristy propped her chin on her hands.

"Could we ask each kid to donate a little bit, or to buy his own gift?" Mallory suggested.

Kristy nodded. "We'll ask each of them to bring one dollar to buy a gift. We could ask them to bring art supplies, too."

"If they did that, we could probably squeak out enough money for anything extra we need," said Stacey.

"Good," said Kristy. "Why don't we send out invitations asking the kids to be early elves at Santa's summer workshop."

"Since Dawn wants to be involved and she's leaving, it should be soon," said Mary Anne, sounding edgy.

"Besides," added Jessi, "if we don't do it while it's still summer, it won't be Christmas in summer."

"Good point," Claudia said, laughing.

"How about this Tuesday?" asked Kristy.

Everyone agreed that Tuesday would be fine. We broke into committees. (I volunteered to be on the baking committee with Mary Anne, but a few minutes later she switched to another committee. I'm pretty sure she did that to avoid me.) Then we began discussing which of the kids we sit for would probably be interested in participating.

By three o'clock, we were finished. After everyone was gone, Mary Anne and I were alone together in the barn.

"Well, I suppose we'll be busy for the next couple of weeks," said Mary Anne, heading toward the secret passage that would take us back to the house. The flat, expressionless tone had returned to her voice.

"It'll be fun working on Christmas in summer," I said enthusiastically.

"Yeah, it will."

I desperately wanted things between us to return to normal. But, clearly, Mary Anne wasn't about to let that happen. She seemed determined to treat me as if I didn't matter to her.

We groped our way through the dark passage and emerged in my bedroom. "Want to go to the pool today?" I asked.

"I'm meeting Kristy there later," said Mary Anne. Normally she would have invited me to join them. Or I would have said, "I'll come with you," and not thought anything of it. But this time we both knew that wasn't going to happen. She didn't want me to join them. She was already getting on with a new life — one that didn't include me.

As she left my room it was as if I could actually hear the click of another door locking behind me. Although I had at least two weeks left in Stoneybrook, Mary Anne was already locking me out of her life.

CHAPTER 9

Friday

It may look like August.
It certainly feels like
August (hot!) but it's not.
It's Christmastime! At least
to us it is. I thought
our Santa's workshop in
summer yesterday was a
success. The kids were
wild about it. Maybe a
little too wild.

You should have seen the way Mary Anne threw herself into the Christmas in summer project on Thursday afternoon. I guess it was the perfect activity to take her mind off what was happening between us. I saw her smile and look happy for the first time since our fight.

During the week, we'd contacted the kids who weren't away on vacation or at camp. Most of them were enthusiastic about Christmas in summer. At noon on Thursday they began streaming into the barn.

That morning, I'd clipped a few pine branches, tied them with red ribbon and tacked them up around the barn to give it a festive, holiday look.

Mary Anne had rummaged through some boxes in the attic and found Christmas tapes that she played in the barn on her portable cassette player. She also found a punch bowl, brought it to the barn, and filled it with a mix of fruit juices (just in case our elves started to feel the heat).

It didn't take much time to do these things, but when the kids arrived I was glad we had thought of them. The twins, Marilyn and Carolyn Arnold, had dug green and red felt elf hats out of their Christmas decorations and wore them. Buddy Barrett had found reindeer horns in his toy chest and wore those, while his sister, Suzi, came with a small, red ball stuck to her nose. "I'm Rudolph," she announced, although it came out "Woo-dolph," because the ball was plugging her nose.

Jessi's sister, Becca, arrived with Jessi. Both of them wore red ribbon necklaces with jingling sleigh bells attached.

Naturally, Claudia put together the perfect outfit for the occasion — red shorts, a green vest over a white T-shirt, and sandals she'd laced up to her knees with criss-crossing red and green ribbon. Homemade papier-mâché Santa earrings completed the look.

This gives you some idea of how in-the-spirit everyone was.

The head elf was — of course — Kristy. She took charge, as usual, collecting the construction paper, foil, and other art supplies the kids had brought. Then she divided us into two groups, a larger one and a smaller one.

The smaller one went into the house with Shannon, Kristy, and me to bake. We picked the older kids, such as Marilyn and Carolyn, Lindsey DeWitt, Becca, Charlotte Johanssen, Buddy, Vanessa and Margo Pike, and Haley Braddock, for this group.

Outside, Mary Anne, Claudia, Stacey, Mallory, and Jessi stayed with the larger group of younger kids. "Who wants to make paper chains?" Mary Anne asked them.

"I do!" cried Suzi (who had taken off her "Woo-dolph" nose by then). Taylor DeWitt, Matt Braddock, and Norman Hill wanted to make chains, too.

Mary Anne told them to take out the safety scissors they'd brought and handed them glue and colorful construction paper from the supplies Kristy had collected. "Here's what you do," she instructed as she began cutting strips of paper.

While Mary Anne worked on the paper chains, Claudia and Jessi got a group busy outside the barn spraying fake snow from cans onto dried macaroni to be made into tree ornaments.

Stacey and Mallory took out the huge batch of last year's Christmas cards Mom had donated. (Mom found them in with the cookie baking sheets, which is not that surprising if you know my disorganized mom.) They took a group of kids aside and began cutting off the fronts to be glued onto construction paper and made into new Christmas cards.

After a few minutes of chain making, Mary Anne began wishing she'd picked something simpler to do with the kids. She thought making paper chains was about as simple as you could get, but the kids managed to cover themselves with glue.

"My fingers are stuck together," Taylor complained.

"I'm glued to my scissors," Suzi wailed.

As Mary Anne unstuck them, she noticed that Taylor's chain looked more like a strip of wadded-up paper. "I keep scrunching the paper together because it won't stick," he explained, holding up his glue-smeared creation.

Mary Anne soon realized that the kids didn't have the patience to hold a piece of paper together until the glue dried. She dug into the supply bag and found several roles of cellophane tape. Once she handed that around, the project went much better. Although she spent a certain amount of time untwisting tape, it was a big improvement over the glue.

At one point, while Mary Anne's group busily taped chains, she peeked out the open barn door. There she saw Claudia running after Archie Rodowsky, who was trying to spray Jenny Prezzioso with fake snow. All the kids (plus Claud and Jessi) looked as if they'd been squirted with snow or maybe had squirted themselves. Mary Anne decided then that maybe chain making hadn't been such a bad choice, after all.

In the kitchen, our Christmas cookies were baking away. At one-thirty, Mary Anne appeared and said, "Charlie is here with the van. Who's going shopping?" (Kristy's brother had offered to drop a group of us downtown to buy Christmas gifts.)

"Who brought a dollar for shopping?" Kristy asked our baking group.

Everyone had, but Becca and Margo offered to stay behind to finish the cookies.

"Our chains are made, so I'll go downtown with you," Mary Anne said to Kristy. She glanced at me. Her look said: *So don't you plan to come along, too.*

Kristy lifted off her flour-covered blue apron and left with Mary Anne, Marilyn, Carolyn, Lindsey, Charlotte, Buddy, Vanessa, and Haley.

Outside, they decided they could take two more kids in the van. Taylor and Matt joined them. Jessi went along as an additional baby-sitter, which they needed, considering the number of kids.

Charlie drove the van to the Pembroke Party store, because it was the only place Mary Anne, Kristy, and Jessi could think of where they could buy fun, entertaining things for around a dollar apiece.

When they reached the store, the kids grabbed the small red shopping carts and began zooming up and down the aisles before Kristy even had the chance to divide them into organized groups. At the Friday meeting, Mary Anne told us that she felt awfully nervous as she raced around the aisles of the huge store (it's almost as big as a supermarket) and made sure all the kids were in sight. Not only that, the kids were grabbing things that were much too expensive, and she had to keep reminding them that they each had only a dollar to spend.

Toward the end of the shopping spree, Mary Anne looked over everyone's choices. Lindsey picked out a small set of dinosaur-shaped erasers. Marilyn and Carolyn pooled their dollars to buy a small troll dressed like a football player. Charlotte selected a glow-in-the-dark rubber lizard. Buddy picked out a small, magnetic travel checkers set. Haley and Matt combined their money to buy a super hero poster. Vanessa selected a six-pack of two-inch brightly colored horses. And Taylor picked a plastic net bag of marbles.

"Good choices, guys," Mary Anne congratulated them.

"I have six dollars from the club treasury," said Kristy. "We can get James one bigger present."

After a few more trips up and down the aisles, they almost decided on a gun that threw off bright sparks when the trigger was pulled, but Jessi reminded them how I feel about guns. (I don't let the kids play with them because guns are *not* toys, in my opinion. At least, they shouldn't be.) Eventually, the kids settled on a posable action figure instead.

It didn't take long for them to pay for everything and return to my house. By the time they arrived, plates of colorfully decorated sugar cookies were cooling. We let the kids eat one cookie each. Then we ended the day with a wrapping party using foil, the few roles of leftover Christmas paper we'd found, ribbon, and stickers. Mary Anne laughed because the packages looked slightly ridiculous. The kids had gone a *bit* overboard with their decorations.

"Now, all we have to do is get the small fake tree from Stacey's attic," said Kristy, "and figure out a good time to surprise James."

"Ben told me his parents said this Tuesday around five would be good because they have nothing planned that evening," Mallory said.

"Anyone who wants to come, meet here at four o'clock next Tuesday," Kristy told the kids. "We'll tell your parents, but you try to remember."

Mrs. Prezzioso pulled up by the barn to pick up Jenny then. Mary Anne walked her to the car. She told Mrs. Prezzioso about the plan for Tuesday. "Remember, Jenny," said Mary Anne, as she helped Jenny buckle her seat belt. "This is a secret. We don't want James to find out."

"Okay," said Jenny. "I won't tell."

"Great," Mary Anne said with a smile, shutting the car door. She waved as Mrs. Prezzioso pulled away.

Stacey passed Mary Anne on her way back from walking Matt and Haley Braddock to their house. "Remember to remind the kids that this is a secret," Stacey said to her.

Mary Anne laughed. "I did," she replied. "But you know how much good *that* does." Mary Anne had seen what can happen when people say they'll keep a secret.

CHAPTER 10

Mary Anne was driving me crazy. It would have been easier if she were ignoring me or glaring and making rude comments. But she wasn't. She was treating me like a stranger, someone she hardly knew — someone who didn't matter.

I had to melt the big freeze or I'd lose my mind. The idea of leaving for California with things between us in this state was more than I could stand. But what could I do? Mary Anne blocked any attempt I made to warm up things between us.

On Friday night, I asked Mom to drive us to the movies. She agreed, and I then handed Mary Anne the paper and told her to pick out a movie she'd like to see. Mary Anne flipped through the paper in about three seconds and then tossed it onto the kitchen table. "There's nothing here worth seeing," she said in a bored voice.

"Nothing at all?" I asked.

"No," she said, heading up the stairs. "Besides, I'm tired."

Then, on Saturday morning, Richard made one of his famous big breakfasts (whole wheat pancakes and bacon) and offered to drive us over to the beach. (I'm pretty sure he sensed the tension between Mary Anne and me and was doing his part to smooth things over.)

When Mary Anne heard this news she jumped up from the table. "Great!" she said. "I've been dying to — " She cut herself short with a glance my way. "I don't think so," she said coolly, sitting down again.

"Why not?" Richard asked.

"I guess the idea doesn't appeal to me after all." What didn't appeal to Mary Anne was the idea of spending the day with me.

Things like this just kept happening over and over. Sometimes it was a little thing — the way she'd look at the ceiling if we happened to pass on the stairs. Other times Mary Anne made her feelings unbelievably obvious. On Sunday evening, Jeff called. Mary Anne answered and actually said to him: "I'll get her, your sister . . . you know . . . uh . . . Dawn."

As if she'd forgotten my name.

I wondered, though, if Mary Anne could keep this up if we were alone together for awhile. Someone else was usually around for Mary Anne to focus her attention on instead of me.

The trick would be to involve her in a situation in which she couldn't ignore me. That wouldn't be easy.

But on Sunday afternoon, I came up with an idea when I happened to glance at the kitchen calendar. Richard had written: *Dinner with Sharon and clients after work* into the box for the following Monday. It meant he and Mom would be out of the house that night.

At the BSC meeting on Monday Mary Anne again managed to avoid me by coming in just two minutes before the meeting began. During the meeting she didn't look at me except to say things such as: "I could schedule you for the job, Dawn, but since you're leaving . . ." She never missed a chance to remind me and everyone else that I was going.

After the meeting, Mary Anne made a big deal about having to go over something in the record book with Kristy. I couldn't imagine what and figured it was just another way to avoid me.

That was all right. I had to get home. You see, I'd planned a fancy dinner for just Mary Anne and me. In fact, I'd spent a lot of time on Monday preparing it. Since Mary Anne had been out with Logan all day, I was able to do this without her suspecting anything.

Mary Anne likes a dish I make called eggplant roll-ups. While she lingered in Claudia's room with Kristy, I put the roll-ups in the oven, tore up greens for a salad, and made garlic bread. Then I set the kitchen table, using the linen napkins we keep for special occasions. I'd even stopped at the store that day and bought this sparkling, bubbly apple juice Mary Anne likes.

By the time Mary Anne walked through the front door, the house smelled great. "What's cooking?" she asked as she entered the kitchen.

This was a good sign. It was the first time Mary Anne had spoken to me in a normal voice for the first time in over a week.

"Eggplant rollatini and garlic bread," I told her.

She looked around the kitchen. "Where is everybody?" she asked.

"Mom and Richard went to a business dinner," I said. "So I cooked dinner for the two of us."

Mary Anne raised her eyebrows in mild surprise. "You did?"

"Yeah, we haven't spent any time together in a while, so I thought it would be nice," I said lightly.

I was counting on the fact that Mary Anne

is too considerate and kind to blow off a dinner I'd worked so hard to prepare.

But Mary Anne wasn't quite herself these days, so I wasn't sure I could predict what she'd do.

"It smells wonderful," she said.

"It does, doesn't it," I agreed, feeling hopeful.

"You made garlic bread?"

"Yup."

Mary Anne sat at the kitchen table, so I knew she wasn't going to run away. I dished out the salad and poured the apple juice. The garlic bread was ready sooner than the eggplant, so we started with salad and bread.

There was no awkward silence between us because we were busy eating. I didn't want to launch into a serious discussion while things were going so well, so I let things go for the moment.

The oven timer rang, signaling that the eggplant was done just as we finished our salads. I took it out and was pleased to see it had come out perfectly.

When Mary Anne and I were almost finished eating, I got up the nerve to say, "Mary Anne, I'll really miss moments like this. We've had so many great times together, haven't we?"

Mary Anne looked up at me with a puzzled

expression as if I'd suddenly started speaking a foreign language: "The dinner is delicious," she replied.

"Thanks, but that's not really what I meant. It's spending time together that's special. Don't you think so?"

"I'll have to get this recipe from you before you go," she said.

"Oh, sure. It's in one of Mom's vegetarian cookbooks," I said. "I'll show you how to — "

"No big deal then," said Mary Anne, biting into the last piece of eggplant on her plate. "I can ask your mom to show me."

"I'm not sure she's ever made it."

"That's all right. If it's in the book, I can figure it out."

I thought I'd cornered Mary Anne, but I hadn't. She wasn't going to be forced to have a serious discussion. I'd gotten her to eat with me, but that was all.

"Mary Anne," I said, frustrated, "I want to talk to you about what's going on between us. Why won't you talk to me?"

"I am talking," Mary Anne insisted.

"You know what I mean," I said firmly.

Mary Anne put her napkin on the table. "Dawn, I can't keep saying good-bye to you every day until you leave. When you're really leaving I'll say good-bye in my own way."

"All right." Suddenly I felt very childish and sort of ridiculous.

Mary Anne stood up and put her plate in the dishwasher. "Thanks for dinner. It was great."

"You're welcome."

"I told Kristy and Claudia I'd work on some ideas for the party tonight, so I have to go."

"I could help," I offered.

"No, it's your party. There should be *some* surprises," she said as she left the kitchen.

I sat there for a moment. My big idea had been a bust. Mary Anne and I weren't any closer than we'd been before dinner.

As I began clearing away the rest of the dishes, I heard the front door shut behind Mary Anne and I felt annoyed. She made it seem as if she were the reasonable one and I were foolishly begging to be the center of everyone's attention.

That wasn't fair, or true.

Was it?

No! I just wanted things the way they'd always been. But how could they be? *I'd* changed everything, not Mary Anne, yet I expected her to behave as if nothing had changed. Maybe I was wrong to expect her to act any differently.

I couldn't accept that, though. You don't just cross a person off your list of friends because she changes location. I hadn't forgotten Sunny and my other friends and I didn't intend to forget my friends in Stoneybrook, either.

Rinsing the baking pan in the sink, I began thinking over Mary Anne's words. It was true, she couldn't say good-bye to me everyday until I left. I wondered what her own way of saying good-bye would be. Did she have something particular in mind?

Was she planning something for the party?

She must be. That was what she meant by *a few surprises*. Of course!

Mary Anne should be allowed to express herself in her way. She was right about that. She'd do it when the time was right — at the party.

CHAPTER 11

Wednesday

For a few moments there, I wasn't sure Christmas in summer was going to work out yesterday. Moving so many kids around sure isn't easy. And one thing I never expected was that James would think it _really_ was Christmas.

Shannon is still amazed when she sees the members of the BSC spring into action. And I think she still finds Kristy surprising. Those of us who've known her longer understand that Kristy is at her most awesome when she's coordinating something major. For instance, I knew, without any doubt, that with Kristy at the helm Christmas in summer would work. But I can understand why Shannon had her doubts.

On Tuesday, as scheduled, the kids began arriving at the barn around four in the afternoon. Jenny Prezzioso and Archie Rodowsky ran right to the box of macaroni Christmas ornaments and each picked out their own. Almost immediately, they began bickering over who had made the most beautiful ornament. "Mine is the best one," Jenny announced, holding up her macaroni angel.

"It looks like macaroni soup!" Archie yelled at Jenny. "My wreath is much better."

Jenny kicked the cardboard box containing the ornaments. "Yours looks like a noodle monster!" she countered, kicking the box a second time.

The entire box of ornaments might have gotten bashed if Shannon hadn't swooped in and grabbed it. "Hey, that's not the holiday spirit," she scolded mildly. "Both your ornaments are nice."

Jenny and Archie shot each other sullen looks and walked off in opposite directions, cradling their ornaments. Shannon blew a wisp of hair from her face and hoped the rest of the event would go more smoothly.

As she stood there watching to see what Archie and Jenny would do next, Mary Anne, Becca, Margo, and Mallory entered the barn. They each held a plate of Christmas cookies covered with foil. "I don't want these to get crushed. Where do you think we should put them?" Mary Anne asked Shannon.

"I don't know," Shannon replied, looking around. "How about in that empty cardboard box over there?"

Mary Anne found the box and gingerly set the cookies inside. Becca and Margo stuffed some red tissue paper around the cookies to keep them from shifting in the box. Then Mallory found some twine and wrapped up the boxes.

I came into the barn from the outside then with Haley, Matt, Suzi, Buddy, Taylor, and Lindsey. Mrs. DeWitt had driven them over early, so I'd taken them out on a kind of field trip collecting pine branches to make into decorations. The ones I'd made the week before were turning brown. "Put the branches in a pile," I instructed as I took down the old boughs from the wall so we could reuse the ribbons to tie up the fresh pine.

Just then, the great commander herself, Kristy, arrived in the van with Charlie at the wheel. When he parked in front of the open barn door, Stacey and Claudia hopped out. With them were Marilyn, Carolyn, Charlotte, and Vanessa.

"We've got the tree," Stacey announced cheerfully as she came into the barn.

"Look what else we found in Stacey's attic," said Vanessa. She squirted a spray can of fake snow onto the top of one of the cardboard boxes, forming wispy, white lines.

"We found this pine scent, too," said Claudia, spritzing a green pump bottle into the air and letting off a mist of pine aroma.

"Mom says that if we're going to have a fake tree it's at least got to smell real," Stacey explained.

"Let's load up and get going," said Kristy, clapping her hands together briskly. "It's ten minutes to five."

Shannon helped me as I began frantically untying ribbon from dried out pine branches and tying up new ones. "Why did you wait for the last minute to do that?" Kristy asked, irritated.

96

"I only just realized a half hour ago that the pines had turned brown," I replied truthfully.

"Well, hurry up," Kristy said. "We've got to get going." She left us to supervise the packing up of the Christmas gifts into a cardboard box.

"Is there anyone as take-charge as Kristy at your club in California?" asked Shannon, giggling.

"I don't think there's anyone like Kristy in the world," I replied. "I'll miss her a lot. Sometimes she's tough, but things get done. The We Love Kids Club could use someone like her desperately. As it is, *I'm* the most organized member, and I don't really want to be the one who has to keep everything going."

Shannon smiled. "I know what you mean. Kristy does make things happen. But, even with her here, I don't think we'll get to the Hobarts' by five."

"I bet we will," I said confidently.

In another five minutes or so our boughs were tied and we packed them into the van on top of all the other boxes. "How are we going to fit everyone in here?" Shannon wondered aloud.

Luckily, Mrs. Hill pulled up just then with Norman. She agreed to take some of the kids to the Hobarts' house, but even with her car, it was a tight squeeze.

We reached the Hobarts' driveway at five sharp (thanks to Kristy's prodding). With Charlie's help, we pulled the tree out of the back of the van and unloaded our boxes. Several neighbors walked by and must have thought we were out of our minds.

Ben came outside to help us. "Does James suspect anything?" Mallory asked him.

"Not a thing," Ben said with a grin.

Mary Anne turned to Mallory. "Wow! The kids kept it a secret after all," she commented. "I'm impressed."

Mallory smiled. "Me, too."

Mrs. Hobart opened the front door before we even rang the bell. "Come in, come in," she welcomed us eagerly.

With barely suppressed giggles and squeals of excitement, the kids scurried into the Hobarts' living room.

"Why don't we go into James's room singing a holiday song," Shannon suggested.

"Okay," said Kristy. "Which song?"

"Rudolph!" Suzi shouted.

"Shhhhhhh!" the kids hissed.

"All right. Rudolph," Kristy agreed.

"What's happening?" asked Johnny Hobart, wandering into the living room, looking bewildered.

"It's Christmas!" Jenny said with a giggle.

Johnny scrunched his face into a puzzled expression. "It is?"

"Do you know the words to 'Rudolph, the Red-Nosed Reindeer'?" Kristy asked him.

"Sure," he said.

"Then just sing and we'll explain later."

With more giggling we trooped softly to the first floor den that had become James's temporary bedroom since he wasn't able to walk up and down the stairs. The den was shut off from the living room with curtained French doors, so James didn't see us coming.

Mrs. Hobart went to the head of the group waiting outside the doors and knocked. "James, are you awake?"

"Yeah, come on in," he replied dully.

Kristy raised her hand and gave a signal for everyone to start singing. As the singing started, Mrs. Hobart pushed open the door.

You should have seen James's wide-eyed expression of surprise. His jaw actually dropped as his hands flew to his cheeks.

At first, he was speechless. Then a look of bewilderment crossed his face. "But . . . it's not . . . is it?" He looked to his mother for help.

"No, James, it's not really Christmas." Mrs. Hobart laughed.

As the singing ended, Charlie and Stacey

propped the tree in the corner of the room. Claudia spritzed the air with pine spray.

"Wow!" said James. "For a minute, I thought I was home again and it was really Christmas."

"What do you mean?" Shannon asked, glancing out the window at the summery day.

"You see, in Australia the holiday falls during the summer," Mrs. Hobart explained.

The kids decorated the tree then with their paper chains and macaroni ornaments. Vanessa dabbed it with fake snow. They presented James with his recycled Christmas cards and his presents.

While James tore open the packages, we passed around Christmas cookies. I placed the pine boughs around the room as wrapping paper went flying through the air. Even though most of the gifts were small, James was delighted with each one of them.

Mr. Hobart joined us, holding a gift-wrapped package. "Mom and I got something for you, too," he told James, handing him the box. With a smile, James opened it and his face lit up with pleasure.

"A Gameboy!" he cried.

"Here you go," said Ben, tossing another package onto the bed.

James opened it to find extra game cartridges. "Tetris, cool!" he said, holding up the game for all to see. "Thanks, everybody. This is an awesome surprise!"

Kristy led everyone in singing, "We Wish You a Merry Christmas." Afterward, we ate more cookies and drank the punch Mrs. Hobart brought into the room.

"I'd say he's forgotten about his leg for the moment," Shannon said to me.

"Definitely," I agreed, gazing at his happy face.

"The BSC really is an unbelievable group," Shannon observed, looking at all the smiling kids. "I'm so glad I've gotten more involved."

I nodded as an unexpected sadness swept over me.

CHAPTER 12

Things started moving fast for me after Christmas in summer. Dad called Tuesday night to say he was sending me a plane ticket in Friday's mail. My flight was at seven o'clock on Saturday night!

I wanted to leave. I was ninety percent sure I did, anyway. But that was so soon. Knowing that the ticket would be in my hands in a few days made my decision seem frighteningly real instead of like something that was going to happen in some still-distant (slightly dreamlike) future.

For the next two days, Mary Anne was as politely distant as ever. This might have driven me nuts, except that I kept thinking about the special event she was planning for my going-away party on Thursday. She'd said she wanted to deal with things in her own way, so I decided to respect that. I now felt confident that things would be patched up between us in the end.

At the BSC meeting on Wednesday, everyone was still very excited about the success of Christmas in summer. Mallory said Ben had told her that James was like a new person. "We knocked the gloominess right out of him," she reported. "James hasn't stopped singing Christmas songs since we left."

I decided that the Wednesday meeting should be my last since I wasn't taking any baby-sitting jobs and I'd soon be frantic with packing.

"Since this is Dawn's last meeting," Kristy said in her most official voice, "I think this would be a good time to invite Shannon to take over officially as alternate officer." Kristy turned to Shannon.

"So I am now officially inviting you to be a full member of the BSC with all the duties and responsibilities that entails. What do you say?"

"Sure," Shannon agreed. "But all I can do is *try* to replace Dawn. Once school starts I'm going to be really busy with my usual activities."

Her words concerned me. If Shannon were going to be that busy, the club would be shorthanded. But there was nothing I could do about it.

At six, when the meeting ended, I took one last long look around Claudia's room. "You'll be back," I told myself.

Outside Claudia's room the reality hit me. I had *officially* (as Kristy put it) been replaced.

Another door was shut and locked behind me.

Mom took Thursday and Friday off from work to help me get myself together for the trip. On Thursday, we had lunch downtown and then went shopping at Bellair's.

The store was already stocked with fall items. I felt hot and itchy just looking at the nubby wool sweaters and woolen skirts and knowing it was ninety degrees outside. It was also strange to think that I wouldn't be needing these things at all. The winter clothing I already owned would be enough to get me through my vacations in Stoneybrook.

Mom was in an extremely generous mood, almost forcing me to buy things. "I won't be around to treat you to these things until I see you again at Christmastime," she said as she pulled a gauzy blue sundress in my size off a sales rack, which were the only racks where you could still find summer things.

Our eyes met and I could see how she felt. "You understand why I'm going, don't you?" I asked.

Mom nodded. "I think so. But if you're not

really happy, Dawn — if it doesn't work out the way you expect — you know you can always come home."

I hugged her. I had the greatest mom in the world.

"Now why don't you try on this dress," she suggested, blinking. "If it looks good you can wear it to your party tonight."

The dress looked great. It had small pearly buttons down the front and it flared at the bottom, which was just about two inches above my knees. Mom bought it for me, along with a pair of new straw sandals and some carved wooden beads I liked.

We got home around three-thirty and found Mary Anne and Kristy baking brownies in the kitchen. "They're for the party," Kristy explained.

I set my shopping bags on the kitchen chairs. "What can I do to help?" I asked.

"Nothing," said Mary Anne, not even looking at me as she took a baking sheet of brownies from the oven.

"We're all set, really," added Kristy. "You just show up at seven o'clock."

"All right," I agreed. "If you're sure."

I took my bags upstairs and spent the next three hours in my room sorting things into three cardboard boxes I'd marked: *Take With*, *Give Away*, *Throw Out*. I had the hardest time filling the Throw Out box since I hate wasting things.

At six, I showered and washed my hair. On the way out of the bathroom, I met Mary Anne. "When you're gone, at least it will be easier to get into the bathroom," she said.

"Sorry, I didn't realize you were waiting."

"No problem. After all, you're the only one who matters."

I bristled with anger. I remembered how she'd called me selfish when we'd fought. "What's that supposed to mean?" I demanded.

"Nothing. It is *your* party, isn't it?"

"Oh," I said. Once again, she'd managed to make me feel like an oversensitive fool.

I returned to my room and put on the new dress, sandals, and beads. I checked my image in the mirror, and was pleased with how I looked. Then I sat on my bed and started writing a letter to Sunny. The next time I looked up, it was five minutes after seven.

I peeked into Mary Anne's room, but she was already gone. I decided to go to the barn through the secret passage. I opened the door and stepped into the dark tunnel. When I was only several feet into it, feeling my way along the wall, I heard the sound of laughing voices at the other end. My party had already begun.

I stumbled along, and soon I was blinking

hard as my eyes adjusted to the bright light in the barn. My arrival was greeted with surprise. No one had expected me to appear from the tunnel.

"Look! It's Dawn!" cried Kristy.

"Wow! It's like you appeared out of nowhere!" said Mal.

"Hi, everybody," I said with a small, embarrassed wave.

It looked as though at least twenty people were there. The barn looked great. Colorful crepe paper streamers stretched from the hayloft out to the corners of the room. Brightly colored helium balloons were tied in clusters all around. Homemade posters saying *We'll Miss You, Dawn!* and *California, Here She Comes!* were tacked on the walls.

"This is great," I said to Claudia, who greeted me carrying a bowl of popcorn. "I know you made those posters."

"Yup. Like them?" she asked with a smile as she offered me some popcorn.

"I love them."

Claudia took my wrist and pulled me toward one of two refreshment tables with paper palm tree centerpieces. "Look," she said. "A refreshment table just for you." A sign pinned to one of the tables said *Healthy Food*. On it was a big dish of guacamole dip with fresh veggies and tostada chips, a beautiful fruit boat cut out of a watermelon, carob and nut brownies, pretzels, popcorn, and a big bowl of fruit juice punch.

"Wow!" I said. "That looks gorgeous. Did you make the watermelon boat?"

"Uh-huh, but everyone else chopped fruit and vegetables like crazy. Shannon made the guacamole, and Stacey went to the health food store for the carob brownies."

The sign on the other table said: *Dawn's Yucky Food*. On it were bottles of soda, candy in baskets, pepperoni slices on crackers, and small party hot dogs wrapped in biscuit dough. I noticed that the brownies Mary Anne had been making earlier were on this table.

"Something for everybody," Claudia said happily.

Stacey joined us just then. "Try the guacamole dip. It's great," she told me as she added more to her plate which was already loaded with carrot and celery sticks.

I took a plate from the table and joined her.

"Not me." Claudia laughed. "I'm checking out the yucky food table."

She left Stacey and me alone. "Dawn," Stacey began, "I've been wanting to say that I think I understand what you must be going through. Sometimes when you're ready for a change and people around you aren't, it's hard to make them understand."

108

I appreciated that. But it also made me feel a little guilty. "I know you've been going through some changes yourself," I said. "I guess I didn't always understand or even try to."

"That's okay," said Stacey. "I did some dumb things." She shrugged. "But if you don't follow your instincts about what you should be doing, you'll never know. It feels like you're groping around in the dark and you're not really sure where you're going, but you have to move ahead anyhow."

"That's true," I agreed. "Feelings are sometimes hard to explain to other people."

"I know."

Just then, Kristy, Shannon, Mallory, and Jessi joined us. "I think it's time for the tape," Kristy said to Stacey.

"I'll get it." Stacey set down her plate and headed across the barn. I noticed that a TV and VCR had been placed on an old chest.

"What's going on?" I asked.

"You'll see," said Shannon.

"Attention, everybody," Stacey shouted to the guests. "The members of the Baby-sitters Club made this videotape for Dawn to take to California. We thought you might like to see it."

"Come closer so you can see better," Mallory said to me. "You'll like this."

As I headed closer to the TV, I looked around for Mary Anne, but I didn't see her. I didn't see Logan, either, so I guessed they were together somewhere.

The tape was a riot. It was a collection of pictures of things we'd done in the BSC. A lot of them were pretty funny, too.

We all looked so much younger back when we were involved in the Little Miss Stoneybrook pageant. And the picture of us with our shoe float in the baby parade was really funny. The funniest picture, though, was of the Mini-Olympics, which we held for our charges. And there were some shots from the making of *Snow White and the Seven Zorbs,* a video the BSC members and charges sent me while I was in California earlier.

There were so many photos. We'd done so much together. Was this Mary Anne's surprise? Had she put this together? I wondered.

The final photo was of us gathered around James's bed singing Christmas carols. I hadn't realized anyone was even taking pictures.

"Ben came by with that photo this morning," Mallory whispered to me. "His father took it. Stacey had to get it in at the last minute."

Stacey? Maybe she'd worked on it with Mary Anne.

At the end of the video the credits came on.

110

A Stacey and Claudia Production. Photo Research by Mallory and Jessi.

Mary Anne hadn't worked on it at all.

Claudia turned off the VCR and popped out the tape. "Dawn, we'd like you to have the tape so you'll always remember us," she said solemnly.

Tears sprang to my eyes. "Thank you so much," I said. My friends grabbed me up in a big group hug. It was wonderful.

After that, someone turned on the music and everyone began eating and dancing again. Friends came to me in small groups, wishing me well and saying they'd miss me.

After about twenty minutes, Mary Anne and Logan came by, holding hands. "How's it going?" asked Logan. "How did you like the tape?"

"I loved it."

"Sorry we missed it," said Logan. "We went out for a walk."

"I can play it for you later," I offered.

"Great," said Mary Anne. "I'd like to see it."

She hadn't even *seen* the tape.

I realized that Mary Anne wasn't planning any big surprise for me after all. In fact, she'd rather be out taking a walk with Logan than attending my going-away party.

That was just how it was. Mary Anne had

separated herself from me and there was nothing I could do about it. It was something I would just have to accept.

"Dawn, come open the gift we got you," Kristy called to me.

"Okay," I said. I took the large box Claudia handed to me and pulled off the purple metallic wrapping. "This is great!" I cried. It was a purple and pink bag woven in a Mexican print. My name was embroidered on the front in black yarn.

"That *is* nice," Mary Anne commented. Something in her voice told me she was seeing it for the first time and had had nothing to do with buying it.

Oh, well. I couldn't let Mary Anne spoil the wonderful party. I couldn't stay in Stoneybrook just to make her happy, either.

All I could do was accept that things between Mary Anne and me would never be quite the same again.

CHAPTER 13

I'd thought I was in pretty good shape with my packing, but I was wrong. On Friday it seemed there were a zillion things still to pack. I'd overlooked the stuff jammed into the back of my closet. There were shoeboxes of stuff under my bed, and boxes of things Mom brought down from the attic that I'd forgotten about.

Suddenly, I didn't want to part with anything. The rattiest little stuffed cat I'd won at the arcade in Sea City *had* to come with me. I was transferring my entire life to the West Coast and that tattered kitty was a part of my life.

By mid-afternoon my room was crowded with boxes ready to be taped up. Most of my things were going to be shipped to me in California. I was taking only one big suitcase on the plane, and, of course, the new bag from my friends.

As I started taping up boxes, Mary Anne popped her head into my bedroom. Her hair was wet. I guessed she'd been at the pool with Logan. "Want some help?" she offered.

"If you feel like it." I was startled by the sound of my voice. I sounded exactly the way Mary Anne had been sounding lately.

I handed her a roll of heavy mailing tape and she started sealing boxes with me. While it felt natural to be doing this together, there was an unnatural silence between us. It was as if neither of us could think of anything to say.

After about ten minutes I felt as though I had to say *some*thing. "The party was great," I told Mary Anne. "It must have been a lot of work."

"They did a great job," Mary Anne agreed as she pulled off a length of tape.

I got the message. *They'd* done most of the work, not Mary Anne. This wasn't shocking news. I'd pretty much figured it out for myself. I guess Mary Anne thought she had to let me know, just in case I hadn't realized it on my own.

This last icy bulletin made me content to work on the boxes in silence. I wondered why she was even bothering to help. Maybe Mom had asked her to.

Once the boxes were sealed, I began carrying them downstairs. Mary Anne wandered off to her room. She must have figured she'd done enough.

"Gee, you packed more boxes than I thought you would," said Mom as the boxes started to overtake the living room. She came upstairs and helped me carry more down. "How are things going between you and Mary Anne?"

"Not great," I replied. "But I don't know what I can do about it."

"I don't know, either," said Mom, lifting a big box. "She'll just have to come to terms with this on her own."

On our last trip downstairs, the doorbell rang. A woman in a delivery uniform presented me with my plane ticket.

As I was signing for it, I heard the phone ring. When I ran into the kitchen I found Mom on the phone. "Yes, Jack, I'd say we're all set," she said to my dad. "No, the ticket hasn't come yet, but — "

I waved the envelope in front of her.

"Never mind, it's here. . . . No, I couldn't get in touch with SMS. It's still closed for the summer, but the offices will be open again next week and I'll get the transcripts then. That should be enough time. I'll fax the records to you as soon as I get them."

Their conversation went on for another five

minutes. It was full of dull details: custody paperwork from the lawyers; medical records to be transferred; travel arrangements for my first trip back to Stoneybrook.

I spoke to Dad after that. Hearing his excited voice filled me with new enthusiasm for the move. Then Mrs. Bruen, our housekeeper, got on the phone. "Dawn, honey, this is such wonderful news," she said. "The house just comes alive when you're here."

"Thank you," I told her. It was terrific to know that people in Palo City were glad I was coming.

That night, Richard and Mom took Mary Anne and me out to supper at my favorite restaurant, Cabbages and Kings. As you might have guessed, they serve healthy food there. It's also delicious. Even Richard and Mary Anne found food they liked on the menu. Richard had snapper in a salsa sauce, and Mary Anne ordered trout with a white sauce. Mom and I ate huge bowls of spinach salad with hard boiled eggs and lots of fresh, summer vegetables.

Although the food was great, Richard and Mary Anne were pretty quiet. I know Richard will miss me and I'll miss him, but at the moment I think he was more worried about Mom's feelings than about anything else.

Mom, however, saved the day by chatting

on and on about any packing details I might have overlooked and about the plane trip in general. She kept the dinner from sinking into a total pit of depression.

By bedtime that night, I was exhausted. I knew I'd hit the bed and be asleep in one minute. I went to the bathroom to brush my teeth and found Mary Anne there.

She was staring at herself in the mirror.

"What are you doing?" I asked.

"I'm seeing how I'll look standing here by myself from now on."

"What do you mean?"

"I mean that I'm used to seeing the both of us in this mirror before bed. And now I won't anymore." She turned to me and smiled sadly. "Want to hear something weird? The last time you went to California, I would imagine I could see you in the mirror beside me when I brushed my teeth at night."

"Really?" I said.

"Yeah. I guess because I knew you'd be back. I felt that part of you was still here so, even though I missed you, I didn't feel too lonely."

As she spoke, her nose slowly became tinged with pink and her eyes misted with tears.

"Part of me will still be here this time, too," I said, stepping closer to her.

Mary Anne's face crumpled into a pain-filled grimace. Tears ran from her eyes as she covered them with her hand. "No, you won't!" she sobbed. "When I look in the mirror now I'll be all alone."

I put my arm around her and surprised myself by crying, too. "Don't cry, Mary Anne, please," I said through my tears. "I'm not sure I'm doing the right thing. I'm just trying my best to be happy."

Mary Anne hugged me hard. "I know. I want you to be happy. I just wish you didn't have to leave to be happy. Dawn, I'm going to miss you so much."

"Me, too," I said.

It was true. I would miss Mary Anne terribly — this Mary Anne, the one who felt things so deeply, my stepsister and my friend.

We wiped our eyes and started brushing our teeth. Despite the sadness, I went to bed feeling better than I had in a long while. The cold, distant Mary Anne had gone. Tomorrow I'd at least be able to say good-bye to the real Mary Anne.

CHAPTER 14

Saturday was strange. I knew it was my last day living in Stoneybrook, yet I couldn't quite believe it. After breakfast, the morning was lost to last-minute errands such as getting my boxes to the parcel post place and returning some library books.

Mom and Mary Anne came with me. Although Mary Anne seemed to be herself again — she'd dropped the cold, super polite tone of voice — she was extra quiet and sort of serious. Mom was, too. I don't think either of them could quite believe I was leaving, either.

We drove down Slate Street on our way home and saw Claudia and Mallory playing tag with the Pike kids on the front lawn. "Could you stop a minute, Mom?" I asked.

Mom pulled to the curb and I rolled down the passenger side window. Claudia and Mallory called a halt to the game. "Hi," said Claudia, running to the car.

119

"I just wanted to say good-bye one last time," I said.

"Don't say it yet," Claudia replied. "We're coming to the airport with you."

"What?" I gasped.

"Watson said he'd take us all in the van," Mallory explained. "Kristy just called now to tell us."

"Great!" I said with a wide smile. "Super great!"

"That's so nice of him!" said Mary Anne from the backseat.

We chatted for another minute or two, but I could tell Mom wanted to get going. "I'll be taking the seven o'clock flight," I told them. "We can meet at the check-in counter."

"Okay, see you then," Claudia said as I began rolling the window up.

We went home and after lunch I cleaned my room. As I worked, Mary Anne came in holding a book. "Here," she said. "I bought you this the other day. I thought you might want to read it on the plane."

I took the book from her and read the title. *Bone Chilling Ghost Stories*. Mary Anne knows I love scary stories and I hadn't read this one. "Thanks," I said.

"You're welcome."

It wasn't the grand surprise gesture I'd

hoped Mary Anne would come up with, but it was something, anyway.

I opened my almost empty top dresser drawer, and pulled out some beads wrapped in tissue paper. "This is for you," I said, handing the package to Mary Anne.

Mary Anne opened the tissue and looked down at the necklace made of beads, colored glass, and polished stones. "But, Dawn, you love this necklace," she objected.

"I do," I agreed. "But I want you to have it so you'll think of me when you wear it."

Mary Anne opened her mouth as though she were about to argue with me about taking it, but she seemed to change her mind. Instead, she put the necklace over her head. "I'll wear it all the time," she said. "Thanks."

We hugged and held each other close for several moments.

Then Mom's voice called up the stairs. "Dawn, phone! It's Jeff. He wants to ask you something."

"California is calling you," said Mary Anne with a resigned sigh as she broke out of the hug.

I nodded and squeezed Mary Anne's arm. "I'm coming!" I called to Mom.

All Jeff wanted to know was whether I wanted cheese enchiladas or a big salad when

I arrived. Mrs. Bruen asked him to call because she wanted to prepare something special. "It will be late," I said. "Tell her I'd like the enchiladas, but to wait for Monday. I'll be too tired to eat when I arrive."

"But it'll only be ten at night when you get in," Jeff argued.

"It will be one o'clock in the morning, eastern time," I reminded him. "I'll be totally jet lagged."

"Okay." He sighed. "I wanted those enchiladas, too."

I hung up and stood by the phone. Talking with Jeff had made me realize this was *really* happening. For the first time that day, I felt excited to be leaving.

The rest of the day dragged a little, but eventually Mom, Richard, Mary Anne, and I got into the car and headed toward the airport. When we arrived at the check-in counter Kristy, Claudia, Stacey, Shannon, Mallory, and Jessi were already waiting.

"It was great of you guys to come," I told them.

"We had to come," said Kristy. "We couldn't let you take off without driving you crazy until the very last minute."

"Yeah." Claudia laughed. "We wanted our beautiful faces to be the last things you see before taking off."

They stood on line with Richard, Mom, Mary Anne, and me while I checked my big suitcase and presented my ticket.

We walked together to the security gate. The officers there said everyone could come to the boarding gate with me as long as they put their purses through the moving security check and passed through the metal detector. (Stacey kept setting off the buzzer until she thought to take off the ankle bracelet she was wearing.)

At the gate, we sat near the plate glass window and watched the planes take off and land. Finally, a voice announced: "Seven o'clock flight leaving for California, now boarding at gate twelve."

That was my flight.

"Okay, honey, this is it," said Mom, putting her arm around my shoulder.

I hugged her tightly and she hugged me back. "Call as soon as you get to the house," she whispered in a choked voice.

"I will," I said, still holding onto her. "I love you, Mom."

I felt her tears against my cheek. Soon, they were mixed with my tears.

"Flight one-twenty now boarding at gate twelve," the insistent voice urged us from over the PA system.

Mom held my shoulders and looked at me hard. She brushed away her tears and then mine. "Don't ever forget that you're my Dawn, my cherished daughter. I know you'll make me proud even if I'm not there. You always do."

I nodded and started crying again.

"You have to board soon," Richard said gently.

I hugged him. " 'Bye, Richard."

" 'Bye, honey. You have a good flight."

I said good-bye to Jessi and Mallory, wrapping them each in a hug. "You guys be good, and don't forget to write me," I said.

"We will," Mallory promised.

"And we won't forget," added Jessi. "I've already mailed you a letter."

Next, I faced Kristy, Shannon, and Stacey. "You'd better write all the time," said Kristy in a husky voice.

"Promise," I said.

"Send pictures and videos, too," said Stacey as she hugged me.

"Okay," I said, forcing a smile.

"I'll be writing for advice," Shannon joked. "Dear Dawn, how do I do a million things at once?"

"Eating right gives you energy," I said lightly. "That's my advice."

"Oh, that's how you do it all!" Shannon laughed.

124

I turned and looked at Claudia and Mary Anne standing close to the boarding gate. There were only two people waiting to give their tickets to the attendant. I had to get moving.

I hurried to the gate. " 'Bye, Claud," I said, wrapping my arms around her.

" 'Bye, Dawn. You be happy," she said.

"You, too," I told her.

Now I stood before Mary Anne. We didn't say anything to one another. We just hugged tight, looked at one another, then hugged again.

"Send me a picture of yourself brushing your teeth," said Mary Anne. "I'll tape it to the mirror."

That made me laugh and cry at the same time. "You send one of you and I'll tape it on the mirror in California."

"All right," Mary Anne agreed.

The attendant at the door looked my way. "You really should board, miss," she said.

I gave Mary Anne one last tight hug then headed for the door and gave the attendant my ticket. Before walking into the tunnel leading to the plane, I looked back over my shoulder at all the people I loved so much — all the people I was about to leave.

With a last wave, I entered the tunnel. I

heard the steady drone of the plane's idling engine and felt the suddenly cold air from the plane wafting out to the tunnel.

When I entered the plane, the attendants greeted me and directed me to my seat, which was by a window. I looked out and could see the terminal. The very first orangish glow of the coming sunset bounced off the plate glass window. I couldn't see in, but I knew my friends and family were there, waiting until the very last minute when the plane would lift off.

I listened for the sound of the final door locking behind me, the door which would close off my life in Stoneybrook.

After a few minutes I smiled softly to myself. I hadn't heard the click or the lock. And, at that moment, somehow, I knew for certain that door would never close.

CHAPTER 15

Dear Mary Anne,
   Hi! I already told you about
my flight (and the gross airline
food) when I called the other
night, so I won't repeat all
that. (It was a good thing
Mrs. Bruen insisted on making
those enchiladas because I
was starving when I got to
the house.)
   I saw Sunny today and
she says hi to you and everybody else. I'm glad to be
able to be here for her. Mrs.
Winslow just got out of the
hospital last week and she's
started chemotherapy for
her cancer. The treatments
are hard on her. Lots of times
she feels nauseated when she

comes home. I know it must be scary for Sunny.

Carol and I are going shopping for new bathing suits tonight. She says the ones I have look too faded. That's probably from all the chlorine in the pool. She says that since I'm going to be a full-time southern Californian I'll need a wardrobe of bathing suits. I can't say I mind.

When I got here there was lots of paperwork from Vista waiting for me. Can you believe it? At SMS we wouldn't even be thinking about school until the beginning of September. I'm not sure I'm ready for vacation to end so soon.

Well, that's about it. I'm headed over for a We ♥ Kids Club meeting right now. I wonder how much chaos has returned to the club since I left. Sunny says everything is going along fine, but you know Sunny's idea of fine.

                    Love, XXX OOOOO
                    Dawn

P.S. Here's the picture of me brushing my teeth. Jeff took it. Don't I look gorgeous? (Just kidding. Please don't show this to anyone else.)

Dear Dawn,

Surprise! Bet you didn't expect to get a letter this fast. I mailed it before you left so it would be waiting when you got to California.

I wanted to say some things to you that I felt too embarrassed to say in person. Like, how much being your friend has meant to me. Even though you're not that much older, I really look up to you. And I admire the way you stick to your principles when it comes to the things you

129

believe in. Knowing a person like you who really lives according to what she believes is something I'll never forget. I also admire the way you're following your heart right now. Deciding to move back to California couldn't have been easy for you. If I'm going to follow my dream of being a dancer, I'll have to believe I have a right to follow my heart, too.

That's it. I just wanted you to know these things. I hope you're very happy in Palo City and I can't wait until your next visit.

Your pal,
Jessi

Dear Dawn,

I am writing to say thank you very much for Christmas in summer. It was super cool. I was very, very, very, very surprised. I wish you were still going to be a baby-sitter here, but I know how it is when you are homesick. Christmas in summer made me a little homesick for Australia. I hope you are fine.

Sincerely,
James Hobart

Hi, Dawn —

How are you? We all miss you so much. We've alredy starded getting super buzy with work. Shannon cant take the amound of jobs you used to take. I dont no what we're going to do. Its nuts. Anyhow, I just wanted to get this postcard to you. Sory abuot the choclit marks in the corner. I was eating a cupcake wile writing

Luv, Claudia

Dear Dawn,
Fair is fair. Here is a picture of me brushing my teeth. I took it of myself so it's a little blurry. Sorry. I promise

I won't show yours to anyone if you won't show mine. (It's okay if parents see it. They won't laugh.)

I hope Sunny's mother is feeling better. I bet Sunny is very happy you're there to help her get through this. It made me cry when I thought of what it must be like for her to be so worried about her mother.

The house seems quiet without you. But Logan is still trying to cram as much fun stuff into the end of summer as possible. And the BSC has been a total zoo this week. Everyone must have come home from vacation early this year.

Sorry I was sort of a pain before you left. I just didn't know how to deal with what was going on. I guess

I don't like change too much, either. But you can count on me if you ever need a friend, because I will be

Your sister and
friend forever
MaryAnne

Dear MaryAnne,

Thanks for your letter. It meant a lot to me. I've received a lot of letters since I've been here, but I wanted to answer yours right away.

I put your toothbrushing picture on the mirror each night as I brush my teeth. It was a good idea. It makes me feel closer to you.

I know you've been through a lot. I hope you know, though, that we'll always be in each other's lives. We've lost the closeness that comes from living together, but I hope our friendship will grow deeper over the years. I talked to Dad the other night. He said something I thought was interesting. He said friendships that last despite long distances are the truest friendships. If a friendship survives it means that the friends cherish each other enough to make the effort to write and call.

I know I cherish you and your friendship.

Love always,
Dawn

About the Author

ANN M. MARTIN did *a lot* of baby-sitting when she was growing up in Princeton, New Jersey. She is a former editor of books for children, and was graduated from Smith College.

Ms. Martin lives in New York City with her cats, Mouse and Rosie. She likes ice cream and *I Love Lucy*; and she hates to cook.

Ann Martin's Apple Paperbacks include *Yours Turly, Shirley*; *Ten Kids, No Pets*; *With You and Without You*; *Bummer Summer*; and all the other books in the Baby-sitters Club series.

Look for #89

KRISTY AND THE DIRTY DIAPERS

The team gathered around me, pushing and shoving. (Except for David Michael. He was standing, arms folded, against the backstop.)

I had a plan. At my house, I'd only looked at the back of the shirt. But here I would first reveal the front of the shirt, which I assumed was nice and blank. The kids would become so psyched that when I turned the shirt around, they wouldn't mind the logo.

I held my breath. I pulled out a team shirt, making sure the back faced me.

The first face I noticed was Linny's. He looked deathly ill. "I'm not wearing *that*!" he protested.

"Dye . . . a . . . Purse?" Patsy Kuhn said.

I turned the shirt around.

The back of the shirt was facing the team, complete with the drawing of a diaper.

"What's it say?" Claire asked.

"Davis Diapers," Nicky replied.

"Dirty diapers?" Patsy said.

"Eeeeeeew!" Margo shrieked, dissolving into giggles.

Nina Marshall looked ashen. "We have to wear *diapers*?"

"Di-pees! Di-pees!" Gabbie squealed.

"Can we send them back?" Linny asked. "Or tell him to put Krushers on them?"

"Well, no," I said. "That's his company name. The whole idea is to advertise."

"Why didn't you ask us first?" Jake asked angrily. "You always say teammates should communicate."

"Well, yeah," I replied, "but I guess . . . I don't know, I figured we all needed the new stuff, that's all."

Glowering, Jake and Linny stalked away.

I felt like a fool. They were right. I should have called a team meeting and proposed the idea. The way I would have introduced a new idea in the BSC. What kind of leader was I, anyway?

**Read all the books
about Dawn
in the Baby-sitters Club series
by Ann M. Martin**

Mysteries:

Portrait Collection:

THE BABY-SITTERS CLUB®

by Ann M. Martin

More titles... ➤

The Baby-sitters Club titles continued...

☐ MG45659-8	#58 Stacey's Choice	$3.50
☐ MG45660-1	#59 Mallory Hates Boys (and Gym)	$3.50
☐ MG45662-8	#60 Mary Anne's Makeover	$3.50
☐ MG45663-6	#61 Jessi's and the Awful Secret	$3.50
☐ MG45664-4	#62 Kristy and the Worst Kid Ever	$3.50
☐ MG45665-2	#63 Claudia's Freind Friend	$3.50
☐ MG45666-0	#64 Dawn's Family Feud	$3.50
☐ MG45667-9	#65 Stacey's Big Crush	$3.50
☐ MG47004-3	#66 Maid Mary Anne	$3.50
☐ MG47005-1	#67 Dawn's Big Move	$3.50
☐ MG47006-X	#68 Jessi and the Bad Baby-Sitter	$3.50
☐ MG47007-8	#69 Get Well Soon, Mallory!	$3.50
☐ MG47008-6	#70 Stacey and the Cheerleaders	$3.50
☐ MG47009-4	#71 Claudia and the Perfect Boy	$3.50
☐ MG47010-8	#72 Dawn and the We Love Kids Club	$3.50
☐ MG45575-3	Logan's Story Special Edition Readers' Request	$3.25
☐ MG47118-X	Logan Bruno, Boy Baby-sitter Special Edition Readers' Request	$3.50
☐ MG44240-6	Baby-sitters on Board! Super Special #1	$3.95
☐ MG44239-2	Baby-sitters' Summer Vacation Super Special #2	$3.95
☐ MG43973-1	Baby-sitters' Winter Vacation Super Special #3	$3.95
☐ MG42493-9	Baby-sitters' Island Adventure Super Special #4	$3.95
☐ MG43575-2	California Girls! Super Special #5	$3.95
☐ MG43576-0	New York, New York! Super Special #6	$3.95
☐ MG44963-X	Snowbound Super Special #7	$3.95
☐ MG44962-X	Baby-sitters at Shadow Lake Super Special #8	$3.95
☐ MG45661-X	Starring the Baby-sitters Club Super Special #9	$3.95
☐ MG45674-1	Sea City, Here We Come! Super Special #10	$3.95

Available wherever you buy books...or use this order form.

Scholastic Inc., P.O. Box 7502, 2931 E. McCarty Street, Jefferson City, MO 65102

Please send me the books I have checked above. I am enclosing $_____ (please add $2.00 to cover shipping and handling). Send check or money order - no cash or C.O.D.s please.

Name _____ Birthdate_____

Address _____

City_____ State/Zip _____

Please allow four to six weeks for delivery. Offer good in the U.S. only. Sorry, mail orders are not available to residents of Canada. Prices subject to change.

BSC993

**Wow! It's really them—
the new Baby-sitters Club dolls!**

Your favorite Baby-sitters Club characters have come to life in these
beautiful collector dolls. Each doll wears her own unique clothes and jewelry.
They look just like the girls you have imagined! The dolls also come with their own
individual stories in special edition booklets that you'll find nowhere else.

**Look for the new Baby-sitters Club collection...
coming soon to a store near you!** Kenner®